TO PLUNGE WITHIN

TO PLUNGE WITHIN

SELECTIONS FROM
NAMMAAZHWAAR'S
Thiruvaimozhi

Translated from the Tamil by Vasantha Surya

ALEPH

ALEPH BOOK COMPANY
An independent publishing firm
promoted by *Rupa Publications India*

First published in India in 2022
by Aleph Book Company
7/16 Ansari Road, Daryaganj
New Delhi 110 002

Introduction and translation copyright © Vasantha Surya 2022.
The translator has asserted her moral rights.

All rights reserved.

This is a work of fiction. Names, characters, places, and incidents are either the product of the author's imagination or are used fictitiously and any resemblance to any actual persons, living or dead, events, or locales is entirely coincidental.

No part of this publication may be reproduced, transmitted, or stored in a retrieval system, in any form or by any means, without permission in writing from Aleph Book Company.

ISBN: 978-93-93852-28-1

1 3 5 7 9 10 8 6 4 2

Printed at Thomson Press India Ltd., Faridabad
Typeset by Jojy Philip

This book is sold subject to the condition that it shall not, by way of trade or otherwise, be lent, resold, hired out, or otherwise circulated without the publisher's prior consent in any form of binding or cover other than that in which it is published.

This book was made possible through the support of
the MR AR Education Society.

For A. K. Ramanujan,
a gentle guru

Contents

Introduction   xi

Transliteration: A Note from the Translator   xxvi

To Plunge Within   1

Acknowledgements   113

Introduction

Nammaazhwaar's *Thiruvaimozhi* consists of 1,100 quatrains (paasurangaL), which are arranged in 100 decads (paththugaL) of ten quatrains each, plus an eleventh. A decad is a paththu, that is, a set of ten quatrains, to which an eleventh quatrain has been added. Each set of 100 eleven-quatrain 'paththugaL' is referred to as a 'nooru' (hundred). The verses are arranged in sets of hundred (nooru) and sets of ten (decad, or paththu), followed by the number of the particular verse—thus, 1-1-1 would be the first verse in the first decad of the first hundred.

Nammaazhwaar ('our one who goes deep'), also known as Satakopan, composed not only *Thiruvaimozhi* but other works contained in the Naalayira Divya Prabandham[1] (the Four Thousand Divine Scriptures), the Tamil Vaishnava canon which is regarded as the Tamil Veda. They consist of the works of the Aazhwaars, the twelve Vaishnava saint poets (often romanized as 'Alwaar' or 'Alvaar', but more correctly pronounced as 'Aazhwaar'—one who goes into the depths). The Four Thousand Divine Scriptures are said to have been received first by the Aazhwaar Madhurakavi directly from Nammaazhwaar in the eighth century, and set down in palm leaves. They are believed to have been lost and then received by Nadamuni in the ninth century, in a vision of the

---

[1] நாலாயிர திவ்ய பிரபந்தம்—திரு வேங்கட நாதன் திரு மன்றம், சென்னை 1973.

long-dead Nammaazhwaar. Nadamuni is credited with writing them down and setting them to music as temple liturgy.

Thiruvaimozhi, known as the 'Third Thousand', forms one-fourth of the Naalayira Divya Prabandham. It begins with an invocation of six quatrains. These, along with the eleventh quatrain in each decad, are 'signature' verses, attributing the ten preceding ones to Satakopan of the town of Kurugoor, and recommending that they be chanted and sung to obtain divine grace. The tone of these six quatrains, and the mention of Nammaazhwaar's name (Satakopan), as well as that of the hundred eleventh-quatrains, differs from the rest of the composition, and suggests that they were authored not by Nammaazhwaar himself but by the compiler. I have not translated the opening six quatrains, but have translated some of these eleventh-quatrains.[2]

In the title of this work, the ubiquitous Tamil adjective 'thiru' or 'tiru', meaning 'blessed', 'auspicious', 'sacred', or simply 'good', precedes the noun 'vaimozhi'—literally, 'word of mouth', or 'spoken language'. 'Thiru' is often used as one of the names of Lakshmi, the goddess of fortune, but with the addition of 'vaimozhi' this name evokes Saraswati, the goddess of speech. In *Thiruvaimozhi* (7–9) the poet Nammaazhwaar ascribes this work not to himself but to one whom he visualizes as the very spirit of truth, from whose mouth it emerges as 'holy utterance'.

~

It has now been more than twenty-seven years since I first began to read this eighth century poet's *Thiruvaimozhi* in the original Tamil. When I am asked why I have been drawn to this work, and why I have attempted to translate as much as I can of its intricate

---

[2]Examples: 7-8-11 (p. 62), 7-9-11 (p. 67), and 8-8-11 (p. 90).

weave of sense and syllable, its evocative mythic contexts and its sparkling insights—not as prose but as poetry in English—I am hard put to answer. Apart from receiving instruction in Carnatic music, and listening to some *Thiruvaimozhi* quatrains sung by well-known musicians, there is almost nothing in my background that leads directly to Nammaazhwaar. My undergraduate degree in History gave me a tantalizing feel of Indian philosophy, that many-limbed creature that swarms over the subcontinental consciousness, but I am certainly not knowledgeable about the dialectic of monism (advaita), dualism (dvaita), and qualified monism (visishtadvaita) which might 'explain' Nammaazhwaar's poetic vision in philosophical terminology.

Whatever I have read and known and heard of devotional poetry from anywhere in the world, not only from the subcontinent, has often given me that strange hair-raising sensation of goose pimples that is characteristic of the adhbhuta rasa: wonder. Of the nine quintessential emotions known as rasas in Indian aesthetics[3], the feeling of wonder in all its forms, from surprise and shock, to amazement and awe, seems to me to be what inspires bhakti—the state of mind usually translated as 'devotion', or 'dedication'. I think of it as a blend of passion and reverence.

A. K. Ramanujan's careful handling of eighty-three poems of Nammaazhwaar[4], including seventy-six from *Thiruvaimozhi*, and his discussion of the historical and linguistic context of Nammaazhwaar's poetry, had made me curious to read the originals

---

[3] The rasas are srngaara (romantic love), veerya (courage), bhaya (fear), roudra (anger), bheebhatsa (disgust), karuna (pity), haasya (laughter), adhbhuta (wonder), and shantha (tranquility). The concept of these quintessential emotions is intrinsic to the classical literature and performing arts of India, and is attributed to Bharati Muni in the *Natya Shastra* (treatise on drama).

[4] *Hymns for the Drowning: Poems for Visnu* by Nammalvar, tr. A. K. Ramanujan, Penguin Classics, 1993.

for myself. At a memorable meeting in Chennai in the early 1980s, this polymath—a scholar-folklorist-linguist-translator, and a poet himself in English—had urged me, and others, to translate from Indian languages. What I absorbed from my several interactions with him over the years was that translation is an excellent way to explore a text in depth.

Smitten as I was with the sound of *Thiruvaimozhi*, as I read it to myself, I felt that it echoed the highs and lows of the enquiring human spirit. Translating it then became a compulsive climb up and down those peaks and chasms. It has not been easy, and I can't claim that I haven't stumbled. Isaac Bashevis Singer[5] has said: 'I have been a translator all my adult life, and I consider translation the greatest problem and challenge of literature.' Somewhere along the way I read Daniel Ladinsky's no-holds-barred rendering of the thirteenth century Persian poet Hafiz[6], in the introduction to which he reminds readers that the word 'translation' means in Latin 'to bring across', and declares: 'My goal is to bring across, right into your lap, the wondrous spirit of Hafiz that lifts the corners of the mouth.'

After I began reading the quatrains and had done some browsing in P. Sri's commentaries, which I found in the U. Ve. Swaminathan Iyer Library in Chennai, I had the good fortune to come across Srirama Bharati's meticulously paraphrased prose translation of the entire Naalaayira Divya Prabandham[7]. The

---

[5] Isaac Bashevis Singer was a Polish-American writer who wrote in Yiddish. He won the Nobel Prize for Literature in 1978.
[6] See *The Gift: Poems by Hafiz, The Great Sufi Master*, tr. Daniel Ladinsky, USA: Penguin Books, 1999.
[7] See *The Sacred Book of Four Thousand: Nalayira Divya Prabandham*, tr. Srirama Bharati, Chennai: Sri Sadagopan Tirunarayanaswami Divya Prabandha Pathasala, 2000.

pages containing his *Thiruvaimozhi* have been well-thumbed by me for the past two decades.

Alwar Thirunagari (Thirukurugoor), a temple near Tirunelveli in southern Tamil Nadu, is one of several place names mentioned in *Thiruvaimozhi*. It is here that Nammaazhwaar is said to have been born of veLLaala parents—veLLaalas are an agricultural caste of land-owning Sudras. Standing in the courtyard of this temple of Vishnu is a tamarind tree. Legend has it that the poet refused sustenance as an infant and walked into a hollow in the trunk of this very tree and sat there in a yogic posture without saying a word. He sat there until he was sixteen years old, when one of the Aazhwaars, Madhurakavi, met him in response to a divine signal, and asked him a cryptic question, to which he gave an equally cryptic answer.[8] He is then supposed to have uttered the thousand verses of *Thiruvaimozhi*. At the age of thirty-two (or thirty-five, according to some accounts) he disappeared into the hollow of the same tree, which, according to some, is the one that still stands there.

I have visited the temple, and seen a tamarind tree there. Not being a botanist, I have no knowledge of the lifespan of a tamarind tree. These accounts arise from the context of the poetry, itself a fusion of text and a context that spirals backwards in time and space, and which is contained in the actual words written by an actual human being, and placed on record. Apocryphal as they are,

---

[8]Madhurakavi's question: 'செத் தது வயிற்றில் சிறியது பிறந்தால், எதை தின்று எங்கே கிடக்கும்?' (Literally: 'If a small one is born from the belly of something which is dead, what will it eat, and where will it rest?') To this Nammaazhwaar replied, 'அதை தின்று அங்கே கிடக்கும்.' Which means, according to A. K. Ramanujan in *Hymns for the Drowning*, 'If the subtle (spirit) is embodied in the gross, what will it eat and where will it rest?' with Nammaazhwaar answering, '*That* it will eat, and *there* it will rest.' Neither the question nor the answer is mentioned in *Thiruvaimozhi*.

these legends express something of the worshipful esteem in which 'our own one-who-plunges-deep' is held, till the present day, in a living oral tradition. In the text of *Thiruvaimozhi* itself, however, there is no reference to these stories about Nammaazhwaar, not even in the one hundred eleventh-quatrains in which the poet is referred to in the third person as 'Satakopan'. It seems likely that these quatrains might have been added by the compiler.

The works of Nammaazhwaar and other bhakti poets, with place names mentioned in them, must of course have been hailed as a godsend by those aspiring to power. Tales sprang up, creating a mystique, a kind of halo, around the preferred creeds of conquering kings. Once hailed as sacred sites, many tracts of land must have been easier to claim and take over. The building of temples followed, and they were soon surrounded with streets, with whole villages reserved for preferred castes and communities.

However, deconstructing the legends about him is not my aim. Making his poetry, which is so lucid in Tamil, intelligible in English without distorting its resonance or diluting its essence is my concern as a translator. The person who wrote those poems, known to us as Nammaazhwaar, was not unaffected by the antagonisms of his age, as can be seen from one verse that speaks of 'idamkoL samayangaL'[9]—which literally means 'usurping religions' and has been taken to refer to Buddhism and Jainism, although Nammaazhwaar does not mention their founders anywhere in the poems. I find this term better when translated in the light of this work taken as a whole, as 'isms' in general rather than as rigid thought-systems, which become sources of unquestionable authority.

In one verse, he speaks disparagingly of the propensity of 'linga-worshippers' (Saivites), 'samaNar' (Jainas), and 'saakkiyar'

---

[9]'Gone are all the isms', 5-2-1, p. 104.

(Buddhists) to indulge in debate and argument, telling them that what they need is simply to praise Vishnu[10], clearly an approach aimed at winning over adherents. This was a time when the cults of Siva and Vishnu, as well as Buddhism and Jainism, were jostling for royal patronage. Emanating from a fusion of Vedic and pre-Vedic deifications of the relationship between the forces of creation and those of destruction, Saivism had produced several bhakti poets (Nayanaars) in Tamil Nadu between the sixth and eighth centuries at roughly around the same time as the Aazhwaars or Vaishnava bhakti poets. The worship of Siva was given institutional shape by Adi Sankaracharya in the eighth century, while it remained for Ramanujacharya to do the same for Vaishnavism in the eleventh century.

Together, these posed a challenge to the two non-Vedic religions, Jainism and Buddhism, which had long held lands on which monasteries had been established. Founded by historical personalities, they had been adopted by kings, and spreading over the subcontinent for over a millennium, these creeds opposed the tradition of animal sacrifices (yagna) central to the practice of Vedic religion. They had their ethical codes and laws, as well rituals prescribed and performed by celibate monks. By creating new congregations, they brought some changes into the caste system, and underplayed, if not actually rejected, the idea of superhuman or divine agency in human life. The idea of karma, which is volitional action, as causation is present in both Buddhism and Jainism. Buddha repudiated the idea of 'soul' as a permanent 'self' enduring after the body's death, and transmigrating, or being reincarnated, into another physical body. However, in order to convey his message of right living leading to a renewal or rebirth

---

[10] 4-10-4, not included in this text.

of the personality, he and his followers used existing symbols and parables of reincarnation.

In most parts of the subcontinent, these creeds were in turn ousted by the upsurge of the Vishnu and Siva cults after the eighth century. Their impact endured, however, with Vedic rites taking on new forms, and symbolic libations taking the place of slaughtered animals when offerings were made in sacrificial fires. One paasuram (quatrain) speaks of towns where Vishnu is worshipped, where 'the smoke from good Brahmins' sacrificial fires clouds the sky'.[11] In another, Nammaazhwaar deplores the practice of offering animal sacrifice and libations of toddy to tribal gods, which indicates the spread of the ahimsa ethic of Buddhism and Jainism, with Vaishnava and Saiva communities adopting vegetarianism. Image worship in temples became the norm, with bhakti poets furnishing new texts in Tamil for chanting and worship. The monasticism of Buddhism and Jainism became the precedent for institutionalized sanyasa in both Vaishnava and Saiva religious centres.

Taken as a whole, *Thiruvaimozhi* reflects a broad view of what the poet saw as the innate human need to venerate, and his belief that the god of the sky, of all-encompassing space itself—Vishnu—was the 'original god' and contained in himself all other gods, and was thus pre-eminently worthy of worship. This, I surmise, must have been what led to the eventual inclusion of Buddha himself as an incarnation of Vishnu, in the Dasaavataara myths mentioned in some later Puranas. Such worship, he declared, was the only way to overcome the result of one's past deeds, one's karma, which alone could explain the totality of any person's situation in life. That he resisted the pressures put on him as a poet is evident in

---

[11] 5-9-5: 'nalla andhaNar vElvi pukai…uyar viN maraikkum'—andhaNar means Brahmin. These verses are not included in this translation.

one set of verses, in which he refuses to sing the praises of human patrons[12], and declares his loyalty to his chosen deity.

The myths that Nammaazhwaar refers to in *Thiruvaimozhi* are the Puranic ones, mainly about the traditional incarnations (avataaras) of Vishnu. The Vedas are often referred to as the source of Vishnu worship. It is striking, though, that he never addresses this god by that Sanskrit name, preferring the many Tamil names PerumaaL, Thirumaal, Maal, Appan, Ammaan, MaayOn, etc. His favourite avataaras appear to be Varaaha the Boar, Vaamana the Dwarf, and Krishna. In his retelling they are infused with the intimacy that is typical of bhakti. Nammaazhwaar uses place names in *Thiruvaimozhi* to give a 'local habitation and a name', in Shakespeare's words[13], to an ineffable experience. From this standpoint arises the yearning for a unified vision of existence—that audacious urge of human beings to mould a recognizable shape of the subjective as well as the objective, to take in all the contradictions and paradoxes, all the questions and all the answers that constitute what Alexis Zorba calls 'the whole catastrophe', in Nikos Kazantzakis's novel *Zorba the Greek*.

~

It is the beauty of the Tamil through which this poet has plunged into these depths, which has made me try and find another navigable current for myself, through translation. It is not a broad

---

[12] 3-9-1, not included in this text.
[13] *A Midsummer Night's Dream*, Act V, Scene I:
  'The poet's eye, in fine frenzy rolling,
  Doth glance from heaven to earth, from earth to heaven;
  And as imagination bodies forth
  The forms of things unknown, the poet's pen
  Turns them to shapes and gives to airy nothing
  A local habitation and a name.'

current: of the 1,100, I have put together 110 in this selection. I found myself going back again and again to verses that describe the inescapable and all-embracing nature of Reality—'that which is'—u*LLadhu* in Tamil, or *sat* in Sanskrit. Between that Reality, which includes and eludes all the forms and values ascribed to it and in which the objective and the subjective are intertwined, and any human language is a great chasm. How does Nammaazhwaar bridge it, and bring that abstraction across to the everyday human plane? And do I dare to leap from that bridge of his Tamil words? Will I land safely on English, holding his vision intact, not encased in prose but wrapped in poetry? Will my rendition have the same nose and eyes, will it have the colour and the shape of its ancestor?

It cannot. There is no question of replicating that alliterative poetic idiom, or that exquisite craft by which every single quatrain of the 1,100 is linked to the previous one by a word or phrase, any more than a child can resemble its parent in every feature and limb and organ.

Something deeper than such a resemblance can, however, result. A poet-translator can come up with a true likeness of the original when they are both immersed in the same elemental emotion: the bhava. He or she follows the original poet into the depths. The direction is the same, but the current created by their movement within that ocean cannot be the very same. Yet, it may happen that the quantity of feeling scooped up in each paasuram can be poured from the Tamil paanai into an English pitcher without spilling, or adding, a drop. And because the English vessels are differently shaped, they may allow themselves to be arranged in a new order, and not in the sequence found in the original.

In 1981, A. K. Ramanujan rose up from the depths of *Thiruvaimozhi* with his verse translations of seventy-six of the paasurams. They have captured the attention of two generations of Indians since, not to mention others interested in sailing and surfing on these waters. It was his considered choice to strap on the oxygen cylinder of mid-twentieth century literary English, a genre of usage that eschews anything resembling the 'fine frenzy' of nineteenth century romanticism, and whatever it deems as outlandish literary flourishes. Intense as Ramanujan's translations are, they are terse, in marked contrast to P. S. Sundaram's lush verse rendition of no fewer than twenty-five decads (275 paasurams) of Nammaazhwaar in *The Azhwars: For the Love of God*. Sundaram has striven to recreate whole swathes of the landscape of myth, along with the romantic/erotic imagery so beloved of Carnatic music exponents and classical dancers.

To my mind, the srngaara rasa is almost too bewitching a distraction from the broader perspectives that Nammaazhwaar also offers. Here, the bracing effect of the understatement characteristic of good modern Anglo-American and Indian English writers cannot be denied. So, I try to keep that oxygen cylinder strapped on as I translate from Tamil. But truth be told, this variety of English has to be updated, in this age of furious linguistic amalgamations and transformations. Let us not forget that four-letter 'cusswords' were one drastic way in which literary English was first freed by D. H. Lawrence from the hold of the style pundits. Most of what used to be considered slang and jargon is now swimming vigorously in mainstream English.

Born and educated in America, David Dean Shulman, the multilinguist of Hebrew University, discovered Tamil after mastering other Eastern languages, including Persian. He has poured out a scholarly ode to Tamil[14] and has crafted several

---

[14] David Shulman, *Tamil: A Biography*, Cambridge, Massachusetts; London, England: The Belknap Press of Harvard University Press, 2016. See bionote on p. 114.

translations, and cautioned me against throwing off my own 'modern' English oxygen cylinder. Go slow with capitals, he tells me, but this creative user of Language (with a capital L) uses italics himself! Such is the irresistibly expressive current of articulation in Tamil (itself without capitals, and lacking even punctuation in many premodern texts, although the Tamil texts I have with me are sprinkled with some punctuation marks).

Indian-English poet R. Parthasarathy's phrase, 'My tongue in English chains'[15] still holds true for many problems of translation, but what is equally true is that by now we have managed to suffuse the English we hear and speak, write and think in, with our native languages. It no longer sounds foreign to our ears, as more and more Indians wrap their tongues around it. C. Rajagopalachari, a translator himself, declared that Indian minds and tongues have received English from none other than Vaakdevi, the goddess of speech herself.[16] Certainly no condescending 'benefit' of the British Raj[17], or of the Anglo-American literary world, Indian English is now a resource for the translator.

As Ramanujan himself advised me to do back in the eighties, I trust my own Tamil ear, and trust my lungs to hold out as I plunge to get at the poetry I want, in the English we know in India. When I have to fish down there for a big experience (and a school of bhakti words is no easy catch), this English cannot always draw

---

[15]R. Parthasarathy, 'Homecoming', *Rough Passage*, New Delhi: Oxford University Press, 1977. Parthasarathy is the translator of *The Cilappadikaaram*, Oxford University Press, 1968.

[16]'English language is the gift of Saraswati.' (C. Rajagopalachari, freedom fighter, as quoted in Ms Neelam, 'English Language is a link language in Social Strata: A Critical Review', *International Research Journal of Social Sciences*, Vol. 2, Issue 5, May 2013, p. 31).

[17]Before Independence, students in India were taught to list the 'benefits of British rule', which included the civil service and the legal system, the abolition of the practice of Sati, the railways, the telegraph, etc.—and the English language.

it up with a standard net, and so it sometimes hooks words with a sharp capital, or an exclamation mark, or a punctuation mark. It seems to me that a translation has to catch the living Tamil, even as it thrashes about in the net of English, before it is brought up to be transported alive and swimming—born again—in a transcreation.

I have placed these verses in the centre of the page, rather than aligning them to the left as is usually done. This poetry is meant to be spoken from centre stage, not murmured in an aside, from the sidelines. Rather like this:

> *...Nammaazhwaar sings in Tamil, seated in the middle of the stage, as in a Carnatic music performance. He is flanked by metre and alliteration. Behind him sit Vaakdevi, who keeps the pitch (sruti), and the translator, who follows him phrase by phrase. She is sometimes given the nod to improvise, even to embellish. Once in a while, Vaakdevi whispers, 'Besh! Besh! Brava!'*

~

The memory of my mother writing poems in Tamil has kept me afloat. Whenever I needed to breathe free, Sury has been there to pull me ashore to the firm ground of daily life that we have shared for fifty-eight years. Among those who cheered me on are Arjun and Sumati, Shyamala and Sachin. It was Bhagirathi who first accompanied me to the the U. Ve. Swaminathan Iyer Library and has been listening for years, as I spout Nammaazhwaar on the phone. And not long ago, when I was flagging, it was Lalita who pointed to the bank within reach.

Sita Anantha Raman, the South Asian historian[18], has been a sounding board for every verse as I wrote and rewrote it, echoing and endorsing certain perspectives we have shared, as sisters. For almost two decades, Mini Krishnan, the guardian angel of translation in the Indian publishing world, has been listening, too. Her view of translators as 'the bearers of a culture that lends itself to the spirit of contemplation'[19] has steadied me, and kept me going. The Kodagu historian and translator Nanjamma Chinnappa[20] has given me sensitive feedback.

Lacking a formal Tamil education, I have been buoyed up by the Cre-A Dictionary, created by S. Ramakrishnan and others. R. Azhagarasan,[21] Tamil scholar and editor of other translations I have done, once presented me with a lifeboat—the University of Madras' voluminous *Tamil Lexicon*. It is now easy to access online, as are the SriPedia, and other translations of the *Thiruvaimozhi*, some with copious commentaries (one is by Sri Madhavakannan).

To the open-minded, big-hearted David Shulman—my third ear, who hears the slightest apaswara[22] and strums the sruti a little louder for me to correct myself—I am grateful. This

---

[18] Sita Anantha Raman has re-examined the Dharmashastras in *Women's Rights and Law Codes in Early India, 600 BCE–570 ACE*, Oxford: Routledge, 2020. See bionote on p. 113.

[19] Mini Krishnan, 'The Second Arrow', *Translating Bharat: Reading India*, ed. Neeta Gupta, Yatra Books, 2016. See bionote on p. 113.

[20] Folklorists Nanjamma Chinnappa and Boverianda Chinnappa are co-translators of Nadikerianda Chinnappa, *Pattole Palame*, Delhi: Rupa Publications, 2003. See bionote on p. 114.

[21] R. Azhagarasan: Tamil scholar, and co-editor, with D. Ravikumar, of *The Oxford India Anthology of Tamil Dalit Literature*, Delhi: Oxford University Press, India, 2012.

[22] A note that is out of tune, not pitch perfect. In classical Indian music, the pitch is maintained by a continuous strumming on the tambura, a stringed instrument set at a suitable pitch for the singer and instrumentalists, or on a sruti-box, a harmonium set at a fixed pitch.

Tamil-besotted sahrdaya has given so generously of his time and attention ever since 17 September 2017, that it 'lifts the corners of the mouth', to use Ladinsky's words. And that brings me to the last word—David's pithy translation of 'thiruvaimozhi' as 'True Speech'.[23]

It wraps itself around that Tamil word like a sElai, a saree, 'a seamless second skin.'[24]

Vasantha Surya
Bengaluru, April 2022

---

[23]Shulman, *Tamil: A Biography*, p. 167.
[24]Vasantha Surya, 'Saree', *A Word Between Us*, Chennai: Sandhya Publications, 2003.

Transliteration:
A Note from the Translator

FUSION OF LETTERS IN THE TAMIL SCRIPT

In the transliteration into the Roman script, which appears below the Tamil original in this bilingual text, I have not replicated the fusion of letters which occurs when Tamil words are put together. In Tamil, a vowel at the end of a word is not unoften dropped when the next word in the sentence begins with a vowel. I have preferred to retain the sounds separately to bring out the meaning. When the transliterated version is spoken aloud, however, the fusion will tend to occur spontaneously, and I have left it to the reader to choose whether they would like to try speaking it to get the exact sound of the Tamil.

Here is an example—the first two words in the first verse of the *Thiruvaimozhi*:

The original Tamil is உயர்வற, which is actually a fusion of two words, உயர்வு அற, omitting the உ (u) sound after the வ (v).

My transliteration retains the two words: **uyarvu aRa**. I have done this to bring out the meaning of 'uyarvu' (which I have translated as 'vanity') and 'aRa' (to cut down; 'fell' as in my translation). When it is spoken, the vowel 'u' after 'v', which is not spelt out in Tamil script, merges with and disappears into the vowel 'a' in the second word.

I have also chosen not to 'double' certain consonants as is done in the original. In Tamil, there are several consonants which have two sounds—ப can be pronounced 'p' or 'b', ட as 't' or 'd'. To distinguish between these different sounds of the same consonant, it is preceded by a 'pure' consonant to pronounce the 'p' sound, or the 't' sound. For instance, the third line of the second verse illustrates the common practice in Tamil of a 'pure' consonant being added to one with a vowel in order to produce the 'p' sound of the consonant:

பாம்பணைப்பள்ளியாய்
paampaNai paLLi aai

Note that I have NOT doubled the 'p' in the transliteration, because it is unnecessary in the Roman script in which the two sounds are separate, and would just produce an unintended emphasis.

ROMANIZATION OF THE TAMIL ALPHABET

Here follows a list of Tamil letters with the Roman equivalents used in the transliteration which appears below the Tamil originals: I have tweaked the available forms of romanization to make the original Tamil, in this bilingual and transliterated selection, a little more accessible to those unfamiliar with the Tamil script, but who have become accustomed to certain commonly used romanizations.

CONSONANTS:

1. In Tamil, every 'pure' consonant (one without a vowel) is written with a dot above it (க், ச், ப், ட்). Below I give the

English equivalent for each, plus two common examples of each consonant being followed by a vowel in some common English words.

(i) க் – k (**k**it**ch**en, **k**ettle)

(ii) க் – g (**g**ift, **g**et)

(iii) ச் – ch (**ch**arm, mu**ch**)

(iv) ச் – s (**s**alt, **s**oap)

(v) ப் – p – p (**p**at, **p**et)

(vi) ப் – b – b (**b**at, **b**et)

(vii) ட்- t – t (**t**ravel, **t**opple)

(viii) ட்- d – d (**d**ay, **d**igital)

(ix) த் – th – th (**th**ink, ba**th**, **th**ought)

(x) த் – dh (fa**th**er, mo**th**er)

(xi) ர் – r (**r**apid, **r**ent)

(xii) ல் – l (**l**adder, **l**oud, etc.)

(xiii) வ் – v (**v**anity), w (**w**ar)

(xiv) ன் – n (a**n**t, a**n**other); this consonant is not used at the beginning of a word.

(xv) ந் – n (**n**oble, **n**ull); this consonant is found only in the beginning of a word, or along with a 'th' sound, or a 'dh' sound. The sound is for all intents and purposes indistinguishable from the other 'n'.

(xvi) ஞ் – nch, nj (i**nch**, or in lu**nge**)

(xvii) ஞ் – gn; not found in English, but familiar in the Sanskrit word for knowledge. (*Gnana* or *jnana*, pronounced 'nyaana' or 'gyaana' when it appears as Sanskritised Tamil. It is invariably pronounced '**ny**' and not 'gn' or 'jn'.

(xviii) ங் – ng – **ng** (a**ng**ry)

2. The following 'retroflex' consonants are found in Tamil, with the tongue going up to almost touch, or actually touch and move on, the roof of the mouth.

(i) ழ் – 'zh'; in this retroflex, the tongue is curled up, does not touch the roof of the mouth, but is squeezed between it and the base under the tongue to make a soft hiss. This sound is characteristic of the language, whose final letter (rendered usually as 'l' as in Tamil) is actually zh. There are no capitals, either, in Tamil. Thus, 'thamizh', should be the actual romanized form, but 'Tamil' has now become too familiar. The last syllable is understood by Tamil speakers to be pronounced 'zh'.

(ii) ற் – r; where the tongue curls up to the palate, close to the teeth.

(iii) ண் – n; tongue is curled and touches the roof of the mouth to make a rolling 'n' sound.

(iv) ள் – l; tongue is curled and touches the roof of the mouth to make a rolling 'l' sound.

Some Sanskrit letters representing certain consonants have been in common use in Tamil for several centuries. These are not found in the *Thiruvaimozhi*, but the sounds, three of them aspirates, are pronounced as some other letters. For instance, s is expressed by ச, and h by க.

(i) ஸ் – **s** (as in **s**ip, **s**ingle)

(i) ஹ் – **h** (**h**ot, **h**appy)

(i) ஷ் – **shh** (**sh**allow, bu**sh**). This hissing sound is to be distinguished from the 'sh' of Shankara (or Sankara) and Shiva (Siva). In Tamil, both are often written as ச, 'ch'. They are often pronounced as a sibilant 's'.

(i) க்ஷ் – ksh (the sound of the 'ct' as pronounced as ksh, in action)

(i)   ஜ் – **j** (as in ju**dg**e) and **g** (as in di**g**ital)

As for the Sanskrit aspirates khh, chh, gh, th, thh, bh, ph, dhh: the double 'h' in the first two, the fifth, and the sixth are not usually present in Tamil, and when they are, usage dictates their pronunciation. 'Bh' is pronounced 'b' *(ப)*, 'th' and 'dh' are pronounced as softened forms of 'd' *(த)*—'th' with the tongue touching the palate close to the teeth, and 'dh' with the tongue further in, and touching the palate more firmly.

VOWELS:

The following are the vowels used with the consonants above. (*ய*, a retroflex vowel, is rendered as 'y' or 'ai', depending on its placement in the word.)

(i)   அ – a
(ii)   ஆ – aa
(iii)   இ – i
(iv)   ஈ – ee
(v)   உ – u
(vi)   ஊ – oo
(vii)   எ – e
(viii) ஏ – E
(ix)   ஐ – ai, ei
(x)   ஆய் – ai, more accurately aai; the spelling of this long vowel has become fixed and familiar to readers in many words, as in the word 'thiruvaimozhi' itself, in which the third vowel perhaps should be transliterated as 'aai'—thiru**vaai**mozhi. But that is not the way this word has been romanized by most other translators and commentators, and I prefer to go along with them in this particular instance. As for the capital 'T', I have

thought it necessary to follow the practice in English of capitalizing all proper nouns. Capitals don't exist in Indian languages, but all Indian proper nouns—names—are capitalized when rendered in the Roman script as part of any English text.

(xi) To distinguish the above long vowel, which has an 'aai' sound—ஆய்—from the short 'ai' sound (இ), I have often transliterated the latter as 'ei'.

(xii) ஒ – o

(xiii) ஓ – O

(xiv) ஔ – ow, ou

~

I have tried to keep in mind several currently existing transliterations of Indian, particularly Tamil, words and preferred to go with common usage. This is why I have chosen not to use diacritical marks (dots and dashes above and below letters often used by scholars to indicate sounds in Indian languages). I am aware that there will be some inconsistencies. Like English with its spare twenty-six-letter Roman alphabet, the pronunciation of Tamil, which does not have an alphabet as large as Sanskrit, is conditioned by usage. Stretching the twenty-six letters of the Roman alphabet to fit all the sounds of Indian languages cannot be done purely phonetically, as we on the subcontinent know that alphabet mainly through, or in spite of, the oddities of the English language—that 'gift of Saraswati'.[25]

---

[25] As English is said to have been described by C. Rajagopalachari.

...taking the plunge...

1-1-1

உயர்வற உயர்நலம் உடையவன் எவன் அவன்
மயர்வற மதிநலம் அருளினன் எவன் அவன்
அயர்வறும் அமரர்கள்அதி பதி எவன் அவன்
துயரறு சுடரடி தொழுதுஎழு என் மனனே.

uyarvu aRa uyar nalam udayavan evan avan
mayarvu aRa madhi nalam aruLinan evan avan
ayarvu aRa amarargaL adhipathi evan avan
thuyar aRu chudar adi thozhudhu ezhu en mananE.

Who is he, of virtue so lofty
that it fells vanity?
Who quells folly, and endows the mind
with sanity?
He, lord of the immortals, dispels
the stupor of lethargy.

Away with melancholy,
O my heart!
Adore his shining feet, and arise.

9-3-9

தொழுது மாமலர் நீர் சுடர் தூபம் கொண்டு
எழுதுமென்னும் இது மிகையாதலில்
பழுதில் தொல் புகழ்ப் பாம்பணைப்பள்ளியாய்
தழுவு மாறு அறியேன் உன் தாள்களே.

thozhudhu maamalar neer chudar dhoobam kondu
ezhuthumennum idhu mikai aadhalil
pazhudhil thol pukazh paampaNai paLLi aai
thazhuvumaaRu aRiyEn un thaaLkaLE.

To adore and invoke
and with splendid flowers
to adorn you,
with water, flame, and fragrant smoke
to anoint, and smear, and touch you—

it's too much,
this pomp and show.

O Immaculate One of ancient glory
who sleeps upon a snake!
How I should embrace
your flower-petal feet

I just don't know.

…alone in the dark

5-4-1

ஊர் எல்லாம் துஞ்சி உலகு எல்லாம் நள் இருள் ஆய்
நீர் எல்லாம் தேறி ஓர் நீள் இரவு நீண்ட தால்
பார் எல்லாம் உண்ட நம் பாம்பு அணையான் வாரானால்
ஆர் எல்லே! வல்வினையேன் ஆவி காப்பார் இனியே?

oorellaam thunji ulagellaam naL iruLaai
neerellaam thERi Or neeL iravaai neendadhaal
paarellaam uNda nam paambu aNaiyaan vaaraanaal
aar ellE! val vinaiyEn aavi kaappaar iniyE?

The city's sunk in sleep,
the world steeped
in sheer darkness.
The waters lie still.

The long night stretches on.

He who swallowed the earth whole and had his fill
of the cosmos
has gone off to sleep upon his snake.
If that One won't wake
who'll turn up now?

Oh, out of the mess of cruel sin that I am in,
who else but he
can set my spirit
free?

5-4-2

ஆவி காப்பார் இனி யார் ஆழ் கடல் மண் விண் மூடி
மா விகாரம் ஆய் ஓர் வல் இரவு ஆய் நீண்டதால்
காவி சேர் வண்ணன் என் கண்ணனும் வாரானால்
பாவி யேன் நெஞ்சமே, நீயும் பாங்கு அல்லயே!

aavi kaappaar ini yaar? aazhkadal maN viN moodi
maa vikaaramaai Or val iravaai neendathaal
kaavi sEr vaNNan en kaNNanum vaaraanaal
paavi En nenchamE, neeyum paangu allaiyE!

Who'll set me free,
now that night has become this monster
that hideously enshrouds
the ocean's depths,
sprawls endlessly over earth and sky,
if he doesn't come,
that red-gold One?

My Kannan,

Heart, here in my breast!
Disgraceful reprobate,
you've left me in this wretched state—
bereft.

5-8-3

என் நான் செய்கேன், யாரே களை கண் என்னை என் செய்கின்றாய்?
உன்னால் அல்லால் யாவராலும் ஒன்றும் குறை வேண்டேன்;
கண் ஆர் மதில் சூழ் குடந்தை கிடந்தாய்! அடியேன் அரு வாழ் நாள்
செல் நாள் எந் நாள்? அந் நாள் உன் தாள் பிடித்தே செலக் காணே.

en naan seikEn, yaarE kaLaikaN ennai en seikinRaai?
unnaal allaal yaavaraalum onRum kuRai vENdEn;
kaN aar madhiLsoozh kudandhaik kidandhaai! adiyEn aru vaazh naaL
sel naaL en naaL? an naaL un thaaL pidiththE selak kaaNE.

What am I to do?
What's this you're doing to me?
Who will ease my suffering?
To no one have I ever complained
except to you.

My eyes have had their fill
of seeing you lying stretched out there,
within Kudanthai's
stone walls.
When will it be—the day that life ends for me
here at your feet?

On that day I'll still be holding on
to these feet of yours.
Just see.

5-4-4

பெண் பிறந்தார் எய்தும் பெரும் துயர் காண்கிலேன் என்று
ஒண் சுடரோன் வாராது ஒளிந்தான் ; இம் மண் அளந்த
கண் பெரிய செவ்வாய் எம் கார் ஏறு வாரானால்
எண் பெரிய சிந்தை நோய் தீர்ப்பார் ஆர், என்னையே?

peN piRandhaar eidhum perundhuyar kaaNkilEn enRu
oN sudarOn vaaraadhu oLindhaan im maN aLandha
kaN periya sevvaai em kaarERu vaaraanaal
eN periya sindhai nOi theerppaar aar ennaiyE?

'That one, born a woman, should endure
such great agony!
It's too much, even for me
to see.'

Is that what the fiery One
is thinking?
He's gone into hiding.

He who measured the Earth,
with those enormous eyes,
those lips so red and fine,
my glossy black bull—

if he doesn't appear, who will put an end
to these thoughts,
this terrible disease of mine?

5-1-5

கண்ணபிரானை விண்ணோர் கரு மாணிக்கத்தை அமுதை
நண்ணியும் நண்ணகில்லேன்; நடுவே ஓர் உடம்பில் இட்டு
திண்ணம் அழுந்தக் கட்டி பல செய்வினை வன் கயிற்றால்
புண்ணை மறைய வரிந்து என்னை போர வைத்தாய், புறமே.

kaNNapiraanai viNNOr karu maaNikkaththai amudhai,
naNNiyum naNNagillEn naduvE Or udambil ittu,
thiNNam azhundhak katti palaseyvinai van kayiRRaal,
puNNai maRaiya varinNthu ennai pOravaith thaai puRamE.

Kannaa, Lord!
Dark jewel of the gods, sweet deathlessness.
I feel you close to me.
Yet I can't touch you.

Between us is this body that you have put me in.

With a cruel rope of deeds long past
you've bound me fast.
To hide that gash that's deep within
you've wrapped me tightly in this skin,

and set me down in the world outside.

9-6-2

நினைதொறும் சொல்லும் தொறும் நெஞ்சு இடிந்து உகும்
வினைகொள் சீர் பாடிலும் வேம் எனது ஆர் உயிர்
சுனை கொள் பூஞ்சோலை தென் காட் கரை என் அப்பா
நினைகிலேன் நான் உனக்கு ஆட் செய்யும் நீர்மையே.

ninaidhoRum chollum dhoRum nenchu idindhu ukum
vinaikoL cheer paadilum vEm enadhu aar uyir
chunaikoL poonchOlai then kaatkarai ennappaa
ninaikilEn naan unakku aatcheyyum neermaiyE.

Every thought and every word shatters my heart.
Even as I sing your deeds, the life within me catches fire.

O my father of Tenkaatkarai
teeming with lakes and flowering groves.
I don't know how to melt and flow like water

towards you.

…when words come…

3-9-1

சொன்னால் விரோதம் இது ஆகிலும் சொல்லுவன்—கேண் மினோ!
என் நாவில் இங்கவி யான் ஒரு வர்க்கு கொடுக்கிலேன்
தென்னா தெனனா என்று வண்டு முரல் திருவேங்கடத்து
என் ஆனை என் அப்பன் எம் பெருமான் உளனாகவே.

sonnaal virOdham aagilum solluvEn kENminO!
en naavil in kavi yaan oruvarkkum kodukkilEn.
'thennaa-thenaa!' enRu vaNdu mural thiruvEngadaththu,
en aanai ennappan emperumaan uLanaagavE.

If I say this, I'll make enemies,
but say it, I will:
Listen, all!

These sweet poems on my tongue I'll give
to none other
than the One upon whose hill in Venkatam
sounds the fluty hum
of countless bees.

For that mighty elephant
is mine.
He is my father, my great lord.

3-9-2

உளனாகவே எண்ணி, தன்னை ஒன்றாகத் தன்செல்வத்தை
வளனா மதிக்கும் இம் மானிடத்தை கவி பாடி என்?
குளன் ஆர் கழனி சூழ் கண்ணன் குறுங்குடி மெய்ம்மையே
உளனாய எந்தையை எந்தை பெம்மானை ஒழியவே.

uLanaagavE eNNi thannai onRaaga than selvaththai
vaLanaa madhikkum im maanidaththai kavi paadi en?
kuLan aar kazhani soozh kaNNan kuRungudi meimaiyE
uLanaaya enthaiyai enthai pemmaanai ozhiyavE.

'I alone exist!'
What these humans deem supreme
Is wealth and property.
They think it's all their very own.
The one Reality.

Why sing for them?

Here in Kurungudi
with its ponds, rivers, and lush fields
is the Truth.

Kannan, in person.

To whom else will I sing my songs,
but to my father, my own lord?

4-10-6

போற்றி மற்று ஓர் தெய்வம் பேணப் புறத்திட்டு உம்மை இன்னே
தேற்றி வைத்த து எல்லீரும் வீடு பெற்றால் உலகு இல்லை என்றே,
சேற்றில் செ ன் நெல் கமலம் ஓங்கு திருக்குருகூர் அதனுள்
ஆற்ற வல்ல வன் மாயம் கண்டீர். அறிந்து அறிந்து ஓடுமினே!

pORRi maRROr dheivam pENa puRaththittu ummai innE
thERRi vaiththathu elleerum veedu peRRaal ulagu illai enRE,
sERRil sen nel kamalam Ongu thirukkurugoor adhanuL
aaRRa vallavan maayam kandeer adhu aRinthu aRinthu OduminE!

You've been side-tracked. Made to dote on some other god.
For if everyone is emboldened
to enter the House of Freedom,
there will be
no
world
left.

Look, it's all his doing.
The magic of the One in Kurugoor
where rich red paddy flourishes in the marsh
and lotuses spring up.

Know it.
Know it and run, everyone!

4-10-7

ஓடி ஓடி பல பிறப்பு பிறந்து மற்று ஓர் தெய்வம்
பாடி ஆடி பணிந்து பல் படிகால் வழி ஏறிக் கண்டீர்.
கூடி வானவர் ஏத்த நின்ற திரு குருக்கூர் அதனுள்
ஆடு புள் கொடி ஆதி மூர்த்திக்கு அடிமை புகு வதுவே.

Odi Odi palapiRappu piRandhu maRROr dheivam,
paadi aadi paNindhu pal padikaal vazhi ERikkandeer,
koodi vaanavar Eththa ninRa thirukkurugoor adhanuL,
aadu puL kodi aadhi moorththikku adimai puguvadhuvE.

Running, running
through many births,
you've danced, you've sung,
bowed down
before
some other god.

Look how many steps you've climbed
all that way!

But up in heaven, they've gathered to give
a standing ovation
to the god of Kurugoor, on whose flag
an eagle dances.

That's the original god.
Fall at his feet.
Enter him.

4-10-5

இலிங்கத்து இட்ட புராணத்தீரும் சமணரும் சாக்கியரும்
வலிந்து வாது செய்வீர்களும் மற்றும் நும் தெய்வமும் ஆகி நின்றான்
மலிந்து சென் நெல் கவரி வீசும் திருக்குருகூர் அதனுள்
பொலிந்து நின்ற பிரான் கண்டீர் ஒன்றும் பொய்யில்லை, போற்றுமினே.

ilingaththu itta puraaNaththeerum samaNarum saakkiyarum
valindhu vaadhu seiveergaLum matRum num dheivamum aagi ninRaan
malindhu sen nel kavari veesum thirukkurugoor adhanuL,
polindhu ninRa piraan kandeer onRum poyyillai pORRuminE.

You who talk of the Linga Puraana,
you SamaNar and Saakkiyar[26], too,
you who argue so insistently—

Look, there he is!
He's become all your gods.

There, at Kurugoor
where stalks of red paddy sway like whisks that fan a king,
stands the lord himself, in all his splendour.
It's no lie.

Praise him, all!

---

[26]'Linga Puraana': a reference to the worship of Siva, represented by the male generative principle (the phallus); 'SamaNar': Jainas; 'Saakkiyar': followers of Sakya Muni (the Buddha).

5-1-1

கை ஆர் சக்கரத்து என் கருமாணிக்கமே! என்று என்று
பொய்யே கைமெய் சொல்லி புறமெ புறமே ஆடி
மெய்யே பெற்றொழிந்தேன். விதி வாய்கின்று காப்பார் ஆர்?
ஐயோ! கண்ணபிரான்! அறையோ இனி போனாலே.

'kaiyaar sakkaraththu en karumaaNikkamE!' enRu enRu,
poyyE kaimmai solli puRamE puRamE aadi,
meiyE peRRozhindhEn. vidhivaaikinRu kaappaar yaar,
aiyO kaNNapiraan! aRaiyO ini pOnaalE.

'Wielder of the Discus! My dark Gem!'
On and on went my pretence, my song and dance.

Yet I got at the truth, and nothing but the truth.
And that was the end of me.
Who, after all, can forestall Fate's decree?

Aha! Kanna, Lord!
See, now, if I'll ever let you
be free

of me.

7-9-6

இன்கவி பாடும் பரம கவிகளால்
தன் கவி தான் தன்னை பாடுவியாது இன்று
நங்கு வந்து என்னுடன் ஆக்கி என்னால் தன்னை
வன் கவி பாடும் என் வைகுந்த நாதனே.

in kavi paadum parama kavikaLaal,
than kavi thaan thannai paaduviyaadhu inRu
nangu vandhu ennudan aakki ennaal thannai
van kavi paadum en vaikundha naadhanE.

Great poets who sing the finest poetry,
those who've been made to sing
of you, by you,
this may not be.

But it's to me you've come today.

Apt upon my tongue
have you begotten
mighty poems!

Through me you sing
of your Self,
my lord of Vaikuntha[27].

---

[27]'Vaikuntha': the heaven presided over by Vishnu.

…the world outside…

4-9-2

சாம் ஆறும் கெடும் ஆறும் தமர் உற்றார் தலைதலைப்பெய்து
ஏமாறிக்கிட ந்து அலற்றும் இவை என்ன உலகு இயற்கை?
ஆம் ஆறு ஒன்றறியேன் நான் அரவு அணையாய் அம்மானே!
கூமாறே விரைகண்டாய் அடியேனை குறிக்கொண்டே.

saamaaRum kedumaaRum thamar uRRaar thalaiththalai peidhu
EmaaRi kidanthalaRRum ivaiyenna ulagiyaRkai?
aam aaRu onRaRiyEn naan aravaNaiyaai ammaanE!
koomaaRE viraikandaai adiyEnai kuRikkondE.

Death and ruin, when heads clash of kith and kin,
the bereaved lying all sprawled out—wailing, grief-stricken.
Is this the world's way, Nature's true intent?

What happens next, I don't know at all.

'Lord, lying on the Serpent!' I call.
'Here I am, at your feet.
Hurry.
Come straight to me.'

4-9-1

நண்ணாதார் முருவலிப்ப நல்உற்றார் கரைந்து ஏங்க
எண் ஆராத் துயர் விளைக்கும் இவை என்ன உலகு இயற்கை?
கண்ணாலா! கடல் கடைந்தாய். உன் கழற்கே வரும் பரிசு,
தண்ணாலாவது அடியேனை பணி கண்டாய் சாமாறே.

naNNaadhaar muRuvalippa nalluRRaar karainthu Enga,
eNNaaraath thuyarviLaikkum ivaiyenna ulagiyaRkai?
kaNNaaLaa! kadalkadaindhaay! un kazhaRkE varumparisu,
thaNNaalaavaadhu adiyEnai paNi kandaai saamaaRE.

The sneers of enemies, the tears of friends—
too wearying to count are this world's miseries.

Are these the ways
that Nature achieves her ends?

O you who churned the sea.
You of the glorious eyes.
Here I've come. At your feet, a prize.
Take me quick, or let me die.

4-9-6

மறுக்கி வல்வலை படுத்திக் குமைத்திட்டு கொன்றுண்பர்.
அறப்பொருளை அறிந்து ஓரார்; இவை என்ன உலகியற்கை!
வெறி துளை முடியானே! வினையேனை உனக்கு அடிமை
அறக்கொண்டாய்; இனி என் ஆர் அமுதே! கூயருளாயே.

maRukki val valaippaduththik kumaiththittuk konRuNbar,
aRapporuLai aRindhOraar ivaiyenna ulagiyaRkai?
veRi thuLai mudiyaanE! vinaiyEnai unakku adimai-
aRakkondaai, ini en aar amudhE! kooi aruLaayE.

They ambush, lay cruel traps, maim and kill.
That's how they keep themselves alive.
Virtue means nothing to them.

But why must this be
the nature of this world?

You, with that maddening scent of basil!
You've got me hooked on you.
You've taken me in
along with all that I've done, and been.
I'm yours now.
Just give me a shout.

Tell me what it's all about.
Bless me, Immortality.

4-9-4

கொள் என்று கிளர்ந்து எழுந்த பெரும் செல்வம் நெறுப்பாக
கொள் என்று தமம் மூடும் இவை என்ன உலகு இயற்க்கை?
வள்ளலே மணிவண்ணா உன் கழற்க்கே வரும் பரிசு
வள்ளல் செய்து அடியேனை உனது அருளால் வாங்காயே.

koL enRu kiLarndhu ezhundha perum selvam neRuppaaga
koL enRu thamam moodum ivai enna ulagiyaRkkai?
vaLLalE! maNivaNNaa! un kayaRkkE varum parisu
vaLLal seydhu adiyEnai unadhu aruLaal vaangaayE.

Wealth—that great, soaring, crackling fire
keeps roaring: "Take me!"
Shouting 'Take me!' enshrouding me
in smoky, dark desire.

What a world this is. What ways Nature has.

Great God! You who are the colour of sapphire.
Here I've come, straight to your feet.
A gift.
Deign to take this one
who's yours
entire.

4-9-3

கொண்டாட்டும் குலம் புனைவும் தமர் உற்றார் விழு நிதியும்
வண்டார் பூங்குழலாளும் மனையொழி உயிர் மாய்தல்.
கண்டற்றேன் உலகு இயற்கை கடல் வண்ணா! அடியேனை
பண்டே போல் கருதாது உன் அடிக்கே கூய் பணிகொள்ளே.

kondaattum kulam punaivum thamar uRRaar vizhu nidhiyum,
vandaar poonkuzhalaaLum manai ozhiya uyir maaidhal.
kandu aRREn ulagiyaRkai kadalvaNNaa! adiyEnai
pandE pOl karudhaadhu un adikkE kooi paNi koLLE.

He held a grand celebration, flaunted
lineage, influential kin and connections,
those in high places whom he had befriended.

He had heaps and heaps of money.
Had a woman, too, whose hair, flower-scented,
beckoned bees, in search of honey.
Alone with her, at last,
in that fine house,
life
ended.

Of this world, and Nature's ways,
I've had an eyeful, Ocean-Hued!
All that is past.
I don't want any more!
Don't judge me by what I was before.

Call me to your feet.
Make some use of me.

4-1-1

ஒரு நாயகமாய் ஓட உலகு உடன் ஆண்டவர்
கரு நாய் கவர்ந்த காலர் சிதைகிய பானையர்
பெரு நாடு காண இம்மையிலே பிச்சை தாம் கொள்வர்
திரு நாரணன் தாள் காலம் பெறச் சிந்தித்து உய்மினே.

oru naayagamaai Oda ulagu udan aandavar,
karu naai kavarntha kaalar sidhaigiya paanaiyar,
perunaadu kaaNa immaiyilE pichchai thaam koLvar,
thiru naaraNan thaaL kaalam peRa chindhiththu ui minE.

Once he lorded it over the whole world.
Now all he can do is beg.
When Bad Luck, that grisly hound, grabs his leg,
his bowl shatters.

The great nation looks on as if none of it matters.

Quick, think of holy naaraNan's[28] feet
now, in the time given you

to live.

---

[28]Narayanan. Note the retroflex 'N' in this romanized form, and the dropping of the capital (there are no capital letters in Tamil).

4-9-5

வாங்கு நீர் மலர் உலகில் நிற்பனவும் திரிவனவும்
ஆங்கு உயிர்கள் பிறப்பு இறப்பு பிணி மூப்பால் தகற்ப்பு உண்ணும்
ஈங்கு இதன் மேல் வெம் நரகம்; இவை என்ன உலகு இயற்கை?
வாங்கு என்னை நீ மணிவண்ணா அடியேனை மறுக்கேலே.

vaanguneer malarulagil niRppanavum thirivanavum,
aangu uyirgaL piRappu iRappu piNi mooppaal thagaRppu uNNum,
eengu idhanmEl vem naragam. ivaiyenna ulagiyaRkai?
vaangu ennai nee maNivaNNaa! adiyEnai maRukkElE.

Tossed about on floodwaters
is this world-blossom.
Upon it, all that lives and moves
must digest
calamity—
birth, disease, decrepitude, and death.

To top it all, there's the hell of
cruelty.

Is this the world? Are these really
nature's ways?

O Sapphire-Hued!
Take me.
I'm here at your feet.
Don't spurn me.

4-9-7

*ஆயே! இவ்வுலகத்து நிற்பனவும் திரிவனவும்
நீயே, மற்று ஒருபொருளும் இன்றி நீ நின்றமையால்
நோயே மூப்பு இறப்பு பிணீயே என்று இவை ஒழிய
கூயே கொள் அடியேனை, கொடு உலகம் காட்டேலே.*

aayE! ivvulagaththu niRpanavum thirivanavum
neeyE, maRRoruporuLum inRi nee ninRamaiyaal,
nOyE mooppu iRappu piNiyE enRu ivai ozhiya,
kooyE koL adiyEnaik kodu ulagam kaattElE.

O You, who have become everything that is!
All that stands and moves
is you.
There's nothing else.
Sickness, old age, dying, and pain—
clear them all out.

Give me a shout!
And take me.
I'm right here at your feet.

Don't show me this gory world
any more.

8-1-9

*யானும் நீ தானே ஆவது மெய்யே அரு நரகவையும் நீ. ஆனால்
வான் உயர் இன்பம் எய்தில் ஏன்? மற்றை நரகும் எய்தில் ஏன்? ஏனினும்
யானும் நீ தானாய்த் தெளிதொறும் நன்றும் அஞ்சுவன் நரகம் நான் அடைதல்.
யானுயர் இன்பம் மன்னி வீற்றிருந்தாய் அருளு நின் தாள்களை எனக்கே.*

yaanum nee thaanE yaavadhu meyyE aru narakavaiyum nee, aanaal
vaanuyar inbam eithil yEn? maRRai naragamE eithil yEn? Eninum
yaanum neethaanaai theLithoRum nanRum anjuvan naragam naan
adaidhal.
vaanuyar inbam manni veeRRirundhaai aruLu nin thaaLkaLai enakkE.

However true it is that I am You
so is it true that you're hell's horror, too.
Soaring ecstasy, or awful hell of pain—
What difference should it make, which I attain?

That I am You I clearly should know well.
And yet I'm terrified that I'll end up in hell!

This grand display you've made, of sky-high ecstasy
Feet, tender as petals.
Bless me.
Give them to me.

…the way within…

1-3-4

யாரும் ஓர் நிலைமையன் என அறிவு அரிய எம்பெருமான்
யாரும் ஓர் நிலைமையன் என அறிவு எளிய எம்பெருமான்
பேரும் ஓர் ஆயிரம் பிற பல உடைய எம் பெருமான்
பேரும் ஓர் உருவமும் உளது இல்லை இலது இல்லை பிணக்கே.

yaarum Or nilaimaiyan ena aRivu ariya emperumaan
yaarum Or nilaimaiyan ena aRivu eLiya emperumaan
pErum Oraayiram piRa pala udaiya emperumaan
pErum Or uruvamum uLadhu illai iladhu illai piNakkE.

For anyone to know
the Constant One
is a miracle of wisdom within easy reach
of anyone.

My lord who has a thousand names and countless forms
disowns all names, all forms.

He spurns
both to be, and not to be.

1-2-7

அடங்கு எழில் சம்பத்து
அடங்க கண்டு ஈசன்
அடங்கு எழில் அ .. து என்று
அடங்குக உள்ளே.

adangu ezhil sampaththu
adanga kandu eesan
adangu ezhil ahadhu enRu
adanguka uLLE.

Steeped in beauty is the treasure that is Isa.
Look within.
Take a plunge into that glory.
Dive right in.

1-2-8

உள்ளம் உரை செயல்
உள்ள இம் மூன்றையும்
உள்ளிக் கெடுத்து இறை
உள்ளில் ஒடு ங்கே.

uLLam urai seyal
uLLa im moonRaiyum
uLLik keduththu iRai
uLLil odungE.

Thought, word, and deed—
Delve into them and quell all three.
In the One within
take refuge.

1-1-3

இலன் அது உடயன் இது என நினைவு அறியவன்
நிலனிடை விசும்பிடை உருவின ன் அருவின ன்.
புலனோடு புலன் அலன் ஒழிவு இலன் பரந்த அந்
நலன் உடை ஒருவனை நணுகினம் நாமே.

ilan adhu udaiyan idhu ena ninaivu ariyavan
nilanidai visumbidai uruvinan aruvinan
pulanodu pulanalan ozhivilan parantha an-
nalanudai oruvanai naNukinam naamE.

'He's not that!'
'He's this!'
Such notions don't touch him.

He's in the earth and in the sky.
He's in between them, too.

He comes in many forms.
Does without them, too.

He's there in all the senses,
Yet they can't hold him.

He is endless. He is everywhere,
the Good One
towards whom it is our fate

to gravitate.

1-1-9

உளன் எனில் உளன் அவன் உருவம் இவ்வுருவுகள்
உளன் அலன் எனில் அவன் அருவம் இவ்வருவுகள்.
உளன் என இலன் என இவை குணம் உடமையில்
உளன் இரு தகைமையோடு ஒழிவு அலன் பரந்தே.

uLan enil uLan avan uruvam ivvuruvugaL
uLan alan enil, avan aruvam iv aruvugaL
uLan ena ilan ena ivai guNam udamaiyil
uLan iru thakaimaiyodu ozhivu alan parandhE.

You say he is. And so he is.
And all these forms are his.

You say he isn't, and he isn't.
And his very formlessness
exists in all that has no shape or form.

'Is' and 'isn't' are the qualities
of his duality.

He is endless.
He is everywhere.

1-1-5

அவரவர் தமதமது அறிவு அறி வகை வகை
அவரவர் இறையவர் என அடி அடைவர்கள்
அவரவர் இறை அவர் குறைவு இலர் இறையவர்
அவரவர் விதிவழி அடைய நின்றன ரே.

avar avar thama thamadhu aRivu aRi vakai vakai
avar avar iRai avar ena adi adaivargaL
avar avar iRai avar kuRaivu ilar iRaiyavar
avar avar vidhi vazhi adaiya ninRanarE.

Everyone has their own way of knowing
their own god, among so many ways.

Each will reach the feet of their own god,
their flawless lord.

Everyone is on a road that's theirs alone
towards a destiny that's all
their own.

1-3-2

எளிவரும் இயல்வினன் நிலை வரம்பு பல பிறப்பாய்;
ஒளி வரும் முழு நலம் முதல் இல கேடு இல, வீடு ஆம்
தெளி தரும் நிலைமையது ஒழிவு இலன் முழுவதும்; இறையோன்
அளிவரும் அருளினோடு அகத்தினன் புறத்தினன் அமைந்தே.

eLivarum iyalvinan nilai varambu pala piRappaai
oLivarum muzhu nalam mudhal ila kEdu ila veedu aam
theLitharum nilaimai adhu ozhivu ilan muzhuvadhum iRaiyOn
aLivarum aruLinOdu akaththinan puRaththinan amaindhE.

Taking birth as countless beings
with the artless ease
that comes naturally to him,
he enfolds himself within the borders
of each shape and form.

Yet undimmed is his radiance,
whole and flawless.

It's freedom.
An abiding state of utter clarity.
A gift bestowed upon the life within,
the world without.

1-3-10

*துயக்கு அறு மதியில் நல் ஞானத்துள் அமரரை துயக்கும்
மயக்கு உடை மாயைகள் வானிலும் பெரியன வல்லன்
புயல் கருநிறத்தனன், பெரு நிலம் கடந்த நல் அடிப்பொது
அயர்ப்பிலன் அலற்றுவன் தழுவுவன் வணங்குவன் அமர்ந் தே.*

thuyakku aRu mathiyil nal nyaanaththuL amararai thuyakkum
mayakku udai maayaigaL vaanilum periyana vallan
puyal karu niRaththanan; perunilam kadandha nal adipodhu
ayarppu ilan alaRRuvan thazhuvuvan vaNankuvan amarndhE.

Torn asunder is delusion
by the great wisdom of the immortals.

Yet bewitched are even they
by the marvels of illusion wrought by the mighty One,
he who is greater than the very sky,
that dark, storm-hued One whose feet spanned
the whole earth.

Never do I tire of babbling his praise.
I clasp him, I bow down to him
even as I sit here.

1-5-3

மா யோனிகளாய் நடை கற்ற வானோர் பலரும் முனிவரும்
நீ யோனிகளைப் படை என்று நிறை நான்முகனைப் படைத்தவன்
சேயோன் எல்லா அறிவுக்கும்; திசைகள் எல்லாம் திருவடியாய்
தாயோன், எல்லா எவ்வுயிருக்கும் தாயோன், தான் ஓர் உருவனே.

maa yOnigaLaai nadai kaRRa vaanOr palarum munivarum
nee yOnigaLai padai! enRu niRai naanmukanai padaiththavan
sEyOn ellaa aRivukkum; thisaikaL ellaam thiruvadiyaai
thaayOn ellaa evvuyirukkum thaayOn, thaanOr uruvanE.

From the great womb of creation you brought forth
gods and sages.
'Go bring forth wombs!' you told four-faced Brahma himself.

You who have created all ways of knowing,
you who have imprinted
your blessed feet in all directions
are mother
to every living thing.

Mother.
That's the form
you take.

8-3-6

பணியா அமரர் பணிவும் பண்பும் தாமே ஆம்
அணி ஆர் ஆழியும் சங்கமும் ஏந்தும் அவர் காண்மின்
தணியா வெம் நோய் உலகில் தவிர்ப்பான் திரு நீல
மணி ஆர் மேனியோடு என் மனம் சூழ வருவாரே.

paNiyaa amarar paNivum paNbum thaamE aam
aNiyaar aazhiyum changamum Endhum avar kaaNmin
thaNiyaa vem nOi ulagil thavirppaan
thiruneela maNiyaar mEniyOdu enmanam choozha varuvaarE.

They submit to no one—the immortals.
Their homage, and their service
he alone receives.
He who wields the glorious discus, and the conch.

For he's the One who staves off the world's fiery malady
that nothing can quench.

That blessed blue, that precious Gem
will come to me.

He'll wrap his very self around my heart.

…caught in the whirlpool…

1-5-7

அடியேன் சிறிய ஞானத்தன் அறிதல் ஆர்க்கும் அரியானை
கடிசேர் தண்அம் துழாய் கண்ணி புனைந்தான் தன்னை கண்ணனை
செடியார் ஆக்கை அடியோரை சேர்த்தல் தீர்க்கும் திருமாலை
அடியேன் காண்பான் அலற்றுவன் இதனில் மிக்கு அயர்வுண்டோ?

adiyEn siRiya nyaanaththan; aRidhal aarkkum ariyaanai
kadisEr thaN am thuzhaai kaNNi punaindhaan thannai kaNNanai
sediyaar aakkai adiyOrai chErththal theerkkum thirumaalai
adiyEn kaaNbaan alaRRuvan; idhanil mikku ayarvu undO?

Here at your feet is one
who knows very little.

But even great minds fail to know
you, who are wreathed in sweet, cool tulasi.

Kannaa!
Because you set free some who clutched your feet
from the world-jungle's tangle of weeds.
here's another who's come to your feet.

Thirumaal!
It's you this fool who's howling craves to see.
Is there anything that equals this
all-consuming frenzy?

3-2-9

கூவிக் கூவி கொடுவினைத் துற்றுள் நின்று
பாவியேன் பல காலம் வழி திகைத்து அலமர்கின்றேன்
மேவி அன்று ஆ நிரை காத்தவன் உலகம் எல்லாம்
தாவிய அம்மானை எங்கு இனித் தலைபெய்வனே?

koovikkoovi koduvinai thooRRuL ninRu
paaviyEn palakaalam vazhi thigaiththu alamarkinREn,
mEvi anRu aaniraikaatthavan ulakam ellaam,
thaaviya ammaanai engu ini thalai peivanO?

Calling, calling out, I stand within
this unwinnowed heap of all my deeds.

Wretch that I am,
so many ages have gone by and I still don't know
which way to go.
I'm losing my mind!

Where will I ever find
the One who rescued the wandering kine,
that Lord who straddled
the whole Earth?
To him, I'll offer up
this head
of mine.

6-9-9

*ஆவி திகைக்க ஐய்வர் குமைக்கும் சிற்றின்பம்
பாவி யேனை பல நீ காட்டி படுப்பாயோ?
தாவி வையம் கொண்ட தடம் தாமரை கட்கே
கூவி கொள்ளும் காலம் இன்னம் குரு காதோ?*

aavi thigaikka aivar kumaikkum siRRinbam
paaviyEnai pala nee kaatti paduppaayO,
thaavi vaiyam konda thadam thaamarai katkE,
koovik koLLum kaalam innam kuRugaadhO?

Wresting the very breath from me, those Five
pester me with their petty repertoire
of thrills and chills.

I'm susceptible, a sinner—true.
But why must you
expose me to their wiles?

Those lotus feet
which leapt over the entire universe—
when will it ever be
that you'll call me, take me
to those very feet of yours?

9-7-5

தெளி விசும்பு கடிது ஓடி தீ வளைத்து மின் இலகும்
ஒளி முகில்காள்! திரு மூழிகளத்து உறையும் ஒண் சுடர்க்கு
தெளி விசும்பு திரு நாடா தீவினையேன் மனத்து உறையும்
துளி வார்கட் குழலார்க்கு என் தூது உரைத்தல் செப்புமினே.

theLi visumbu kadithu Odi theevaLaiththu minn ilagum
oLimukilkaaL! thirumoozhi kaLaththu uRaiyum oNchudarkku
theLi visumbu thiru naadaa theevinaiyEn manaththu uRaiyum
thuLivaargat kuzhalaarkku en thoothu uraiththal cheppuminE.

Racing in the limpid sky,
ringed with fire, winged with lightning
O you luminous clouds.
Hasten to the radiant flame
that glows in the town
of the sacred discus.

To that clear space that fills, unsought,
this wrongdoer's heart.
To the lord whose flowing locks drip nectar
take my plea.

2-1-4

க டலும் மலையும் விசும்பும் துழாய் எம்போல்
சுடர் கொள் இராப்பகல் துஞ்சாயால் தண் வாடாய்!
அடல் கொள் படை ஆழி அம்மானைக்காண்பான் நீ
உடலம் நோய் உற்றாயோ ஊழிதோர் ஊழியே?

kadalum malaiyum visumbum thuzhaai empOl,
sudar koL iraappakal thunchaayaal thaN vaadaai!
adal koL padai aazhi ammaanaik kaaNbaan nI,
udalam nOi uRRaayO oozithOR oozhiyE?

Cleaving ocean and mountain and sky
like a wildfire that's blazing night and day
O Wind, you're sleepless and cold!

Age after age, how you've hankered to behold
that terrible discus-hurling Lord!

Aren't you sick of that ache by now?

1-9-6

மாயன் என் நெஞ்சில் உள்ளான் மற்றும் எவர்க்கும் அதுவே
காயமும் சீவனும் தானே காலும் எரியும் அவனே
சேயன் அணியன் எவர்க்கும் சி ந்தைக்கும் கோசரம் அல்லன்
தூயன் துயக்கன் மயக்கன் என்னுடை தோளி ஞையானே மயக்கன்.

maayan ennenchil uLLaan maRRum yevarkkum athuvE,
kaayamum seevanum thaanE kaalum eriyum avanE,
chEyan aNiyan yevarkkum chindhaikkum kOsaramallan,
thUyan thuyakkan mayakkan ennudaith thOLiNai yaanE mayakkan.

In my breast is a wizard.
He is in everyone too, as their body and as their very life.
He's Wind, he's Fire.
He is both out of range and close at hand for everyone.
Thought can't reach him,
the unsullied One,

the charmer, the trickster
who rides upon
my shoulders.

1-7-7

யான் ஒட்டி என்னுள் இருத்துவன் என்றிலன்
தான் ஒட்டி வந்து என் தனி நெஞ்சை வஞ்சித்து
ஊன் ஒட்டி நின்று என் உயிரில் கலந்து இயல்
வான் ஒட்டுமோ இனி என்னை நெகிழ்க்கவே.

yaanotti ennuL iruththuvan enRilan,
thaanottivandhu en thani nenjai vanjiththu,
oonotti ninRu en uyiril kalandhu, iyal
vaanottumO ini ennai negizh kavE.

I didn't cling to him, or try to pull him
into me.
It was he who came and stuck to me,
slyly invading
my freedom-loving breast.

Attaching himself to my flesh,
he's oozed into
my very life.

Will he now fuse with the sky
and melt me
into it?

7-8-2

அம் கள் மலர் தண் துழாய் முடி அச்சுதனே[29] *அருளாய்*
திங்களும் ஞாயிரும் ஆய் செழும் பல் சுடர் ஆய் இருள் ஆய்
பொங்கு பொழி மழை ஆய் புகழ் ஆய் பழி ஆய் பின்னும் நீ
வெம் கண் வெம் கூற்றமும் ஆம் இவை என்ன விசித்திரமே!

am kaL malar thaN thuzhaai mudi achchuthanE! aruLaai,
thingaLum NYaayiRumaay chezhum pal chudaraai iruLaai,
pongu pozhimazhai aai pukhazaai pazhiyaai pinnum nee,
vem kaN vem kooRRamum aam ivai enna vichiththiramE!

Heady with nectar is the lovely lily
in your crown of cool tulasi
O deathless One.[30]

It's you who deigns to be
the moon. The sun. Light's bounty.
Darkness.
Foaming, copious rain.
Fame, and blame.

And then it's you again:
fiery-eyed, cruel death.

What are these baffling mysteries?

---

[29] Achchuthan: he who is immortal; one of the names of Vishnu.
[30] 'tulasi': Indian basil (*Occimum tenuiflorum*), a prized common herb, and held sacred to Vishnu.

5-6-1

கடல் ஞாலம் செய்தேனும் யானே என்னும்
கடல் ஞாலம் ஆவேனும் யானே என்னும்
கடல் ஞாலம் கொண்டேனும் யானே என்னும்
கடல் ஞாலம் கீண்டேனும் யானே என்னும்
கடல் ஞாலம் உண்டேனும் யானே என்னும்
கடல் ஞாலத்து ஈசன் வந்து ஏறக்கொலோ?
கடல் ஞாலத்தீர்க்கு இவை என் சொல்லுகேன்?
கடல் ஞாலத்து என் மகள் கற்கின்றவே?

kadal nyaalam seithEnum yaanE ennum
kadal nyaalam aavEnum yaanE ennum
kadal nyaalam koNdEnum yaanE ennum
kadal nyaalam keeNdEnum yaanE ennum
kadal nyaalam uNdEnum yaanE ennum
kadal nyaalaththu eesan vanthu ERakkolO?
kadal nyaalaththeerkku ivaiyen sollugEn?
kadal nyaalaththu en magaL kaRkinRavE?

What's got into this girl of mine?
'This ocean, this earth—I made them!'
she says.
'I am all these seas, and all these lands.
I took over ocean, earth, and all besides
in three strides.
I've downed this universe in one swallow.
It's in me, now,
inside.'

Who makes her say this? Could it be
that One—

he who's the lord of land and sea?
Has he possessed her?

Oh, all you creatures of the sea!
People of every land!
How can I make you understand
my child's ecstasy?

5-6-4

செய்கின்ற கிதி எல்லாம் யானே என்னும்
செய்வான் நின்றன களும் யானே என்னும்
செய்து முன் இற ந்தவும் யானே என்னும்
செய்கை பயன் உண்பேன் என்னும் யானே என்னும்
செய்வார்களை செய்வேனும் யானே என்னும்
செய்ய கமளக்கண்ணன் ஏறக்கொலோ?
செய்ய உலகத்திர்க்கு இவை என் சொல்லுகேன்
செய்ய கனி வாய் இள மான் திறத்தே ?

seikinRa kithi ellaam yaanE ennum
seivaan ninRanakaLum yaanE ennum
seithumun iRandhavum yaanE ennum
seigai payan uNbenum yaanE ennum
seivaargaLaich chei vEnum yaanE ennum
seiya kamalak kaNNaN ERak kolO?
seiya ulakaththeerkku ivai en sollugEn
seiya kanivaai iLa maan thiRaththE?

'Everything that happens is me. Everything that's ever happened is me.
I'm everything that'll happen, eventually.
I make things happen.
All happenings are a feast for me.'

What's happening to my tender young doe?
She's obsessed.
What has Lotus-Eyes been up to with my girl,
with lips like red berries?
She is by love possessed!

Good people, how can I say
what I should hope for, or fear?

4-6-3

இது காண்மின் அன்னைமீர்! இக் கட்டுவிச்சி சொல் கொண்டு நீர்
எது வானும் செய்து அங்கோர் கள்ளும் இறைச்சியும் தூவேன்மின்
மதுவர் துழாய் முடி மாயப்பிரான் கழல் வாழ்த்தினால்
அதுவே இவள் உற்ற நோய்க்கும் அருமருந்தாகுமே.

idhu kaaNmin annaimeer! ik kattuvichchi soRkondu, neer
edhuvaanum seidhu angOr kaLLum iRaichchiyum thoovEnmin,
madhuvaar thuzhaai mudi maayappiraan kazhal vaazhththinaal,
adhuvE ivaLuRRa nOykkum arumarunNthaagumE.

Look here, all you mothers!
Don't do whatever this sorceress says,
splashing toddy, scattering bits of meat
here, there, and everywhere!

Just praise the feet
of the Enchanter,
the one with basil-scented hair.

That's all you need to treat
the malady that torments her.
It is the perfect cure.

4-6-2

*திசை கின்றதே இவள் நோய் இது மிக்க பெரும் தெய்வம்
இசைப்பு இன்றி நீர் அணங்கு ஆடும் இளந்தெய்வம் அன்று இது
திசைப்பு இன்றியே சங்கு சக்கரம் என்று இவள் கேட்க நீர்
இசை கிற்றாகில், நன்றே இல் பெறும், இது காண்மினே.*

thisai kinRathE ivaL nOi idhu mikka perun dhaivam,
isaippu inRi neer aNaNgu aadum iLandhaivam anRu ithu,
thisaippu inRiyE sangu sakkara enRu ivaL kEtka, neer
isaikkiRRaagil nanRE il peRum ithu kaaNminE.

This sickness that's befuddling her—
it's a great big god who's possessing her.
Not some petty godling that's obsessing her.

Clearly, steadily, keep murmuring to her:
'Conch…. Discus…. Conch…. Discus…. Conch…. Discus….'
Those words are music to her ear.

Watch them healing her.

...asking the way...

5-10-7

ஒண் சுடரோடு இருளுமாய் நின்ற ஆறும் உண்மை யோடு இன்மையாய்
வந்து என்
கண்கொள்ளா வகை நீ கரந்து என்னை செய்கின்றன
எண் கொள் சிந்தையுள் நைகின்றேன் என் கரிய மாணிக்கமே! என்
கண்கட்குத்
திண் கொள்ள ஒரு நாள் அருளாய், ஒரு நாள் அருளாய், உன் திரு உருவே.

oN sudarOdu iruLumaai ninRavaaRum uNmaiyOdu inmai aai vandhu
enkaN koLLaavagai nee karandhu ennai cheikinRana
eNkoL sindhaiyuL naikinREN en kariya maaNikkamE! en kaNkatku
thiN koLLa orunaaL aruLaai un thiru uruvE.

In flame you stand as darkness.
As truth you come to me, along with untruth.
And my eyes can't hold you.

I'm torn to shreds by countless thoughts.

My dark Gem!
Be so good as to allow my eyes
to feast, one day.

Fill me to the brim
with your true form.

6-3-1

நல்குரவும் செல்வும் நரகும் சுவர்க்கமும் ஆய்
வெல்பகையும் நட்பும் விடமும் அமுதமும் ஆய்
பல்வகையும் பரந்த பெருமான் என்னை ஆள்வானாய்
செல்வம் மல்கு குடித் திருவிண்ணகர் கண்டேனே.

nalkuravum selvum naragum suvargamum aai
vel pagaiyum natpum vidamum amuthamum aai
palvagaiyum parandha perumaan ennai aaLvaanai
selvam malgu kudi thiruviNNagar kandEnE.

As privation and prosperity, as hell and heaven,
As enmity and amity, as venom and elixir
he holds sway, in many ways,
the One who reigns over me.

Among all those who thrive in the heavenly city
of Tiruvinnagar
it is He I see.

6-3-2

கண்ட இன்பம் துன்பம் கலக்கங்களும் தேற்றமும் ஆய்
தண்டமும் தண்மையும் தழலும் நிழலும் ஆய்
கண்டு கோடற்கு அரிய பெருமான் என்னை ஆள்வான் ஊர்
தெண் திரைப் புனல் சூழ் திருவிண்ணகர் நல் நகரே.

kanda inbam thunbam kalakkangaLum thEtramum aai
dhandamum thaNmaiyum thazhalum nizhalumaai
kandu kOdaRku ariya perumaan ennai aaLvaan oor
then thirai punalsoozh thiruviNNagar nal nagarE.

> He's seen as bliss and misery,
> as turbulence and tranquility.
> As retribution and clemency,
> burning light,
> cold shadow.

Even for those who see him he is hard to know.

> The Great One who rules over me
> dwells in a town ringed around
> with cool streams—

> Tiruvinnagar,
> city of felicity.

6-3-3

நகரமும் நாடுகளும் ஞானமும் மூடமும் ஆய்
நிகர் இல் சூழ் சுடர் ஆய் இருள் ஆய் நிலன் ஆய் விசும்பாய்
சிகர மாடங்கள் சூழ் திருவிண்ணகர் சேர்ந்த பிரான்
புகர் கொள் கீர்த்தி அல்லால் இல்லை யாவர்க்கும் புண்ணியமே.

nagaramum naadugaLum nyaanamum moodamum aai
nigaril soozh sudaraai iruLaai nilan aai visumpaai
sigara maadangaL soozh thiruviNNagar chErndha piraan
pugarkoL keerththi allaal illai yaavarkkum puNNiyamE.

In city and country, in wisdom and folly,
in boundless, all-encompassing light,
in darkness,
in the earth and in the firmament above,

and here
in Tiruvinnagar,
in the midst of turreted mansions
dwells the lord.

Those who find their way into his glory—
they're the blessed ones.

7-8-1

மாயா வாமன னே மதுசூதா நீ அருளாய்
தீ யாய் நீராய் நிலன் ஆய் விசும்பு ஆய் கால் ஆய்
தாய் ஆய் தந்தையாய் மக்களாய் மற்றுமாய் முற்றும் ஆய்
நீ ஆய் நீ நின்றவாறு இவை என்ன நியாயங்களே!

maayaa vaamananE madhuchoodhaa! nee aruLaai!
thee aai neeraai nilanaai visumbaai kaalaai,
thaai aai thandhai aai makkaLaai maRRumaai muRRumaai,
nee aai nee ninRavaaRu ivai enna niyaayangaLE!

Vamana[31], you little sorcerer!
You who slew Madhu![32]
You deign to appear
as fire, water, earth, sky.

As death, too.

As mother, father, children, and all the rest.
All of it, the whole of it,
is just you.

---

[31]'Vamana': this fifth incarnation of Vishnu, a dwarf, was granted as much land as he could measure in three steps by King Mahabali, who though generous and righteous was inclined to pride. At once Vamana grew to an immense size, placed one step on the earth and the other in the sky, and asked where he should put his third step, upon which the chastened Mahabali offered his own head for him to place his foot.

[32]Madhu, along with Kaustubha, was one of the two demons who took away the Vedas from Brahma, did penance and obtained the boon of choosing his own time of death. He was subdued and finally slain by Vishnu (Madhusudana: he who slew Madhu).

But when you stand here,
as your own
Self,
where need is there
for all of these?

7-8-3

சித்திரத் தேர் வலவா! திருசக்கரத்தாய், அருளாய்,
எத்தனை ஓர் உகமும் அவை ஆய் அவற்றுள் இயலும்
ஒத்த ஒண் பல் பொருள்கள் உலப்பு இல்லன ஆய் வியவு ஆய்,
வித்தகத்தாய் நிற்றி நீ இவை என்ன விடமங்களே!

chiththira thErvalavaa thiru chakkaraththaai! aruLaai,
eththanaiyOr ugamum avai aay avaRRuL iyalum,
oththa oN pal poruLkaL ulappu illana aai viyavu aai,
viththagaththaai nitRi nee ivai enna vidamangaLE!

O hero of marvels, who drives this world-chariot!
You of the great discus.

Have the grace to tell me, please:
As how many aeons have you
taken form?
And as how many forms
do you live and move in them?
How many escape extinction? How many disperse?

O Intelligence Manifest!
Why all these mischievous tricks?

7-8-4

கள் அவிழ் தாமரைகண் கண்ணனே! எனக்கு ஒன்று அருளாய்.
உள்ளதும் இல்லதுமாய் உலப்பு இல்லன் ஆய், வியவு ஆய்
வெள்ளை தடம் கடலும் விட நாக அணைமேல் மருவி
உள்ளப் பல் யோகு செய்தி இவை என்ன உபாயங்களே.

kaL avizh thaamaraikkaN kaNNaNE! enakkonRu aruLaai,
uLLadhum illadhumaai ulappu illan aai, viyavu aai,
veLLaith thadam kadaluL vida naaga aNai mEl maruvi,
uLLa pal yOgu cheithivai enna upaayangaLE!

Kannaa of the lotus eyes that spill dizzying mischief!
Will you explain how it is that you're both
everything, and nothing?
Yet never cease to be, and take so many shapes?

You're both the white, wide ocean
and the One who lolls upon
the lethal snake-bed spread on it!

Many are the yogic feats that you pull off.
But why these stratagems?
What are they for?

7-8-5

பாசங்கள் நீக்கி என்னை உனக்கே அறக்கொண்டிட்டு நீ
வாச மலர்த் தண் துழாழ் முடி மாயவனே நீ அருளாய்
காயமும் சீவனும் ஆய் கழிவு ஆய் பிறப்பு ஆய் பின்னும் நீ
மாயங்கள் செய்து வைத்தி இவை என்ன மயக்கு களே.

paasangaL neekki ennai unakkE aRak koNdittu, nee
vaasa malar thaN thuzhaai mudi maayavanE!aruLaai,
kaayamum jeevanum aai kazhivaai piRappaai pinnum nee,
maayangaL cheydhuvaiththi ivaiyenna mayakkukkaLE!

Stripping me of cravings, seizing hold of me
you made me your own.
O Conjurer, crowned with sweet-smelling flowers and cool basil!

Be so good as to tell me this:
You've become
this body, this life.
You're that which is cast off.
What's born again.
By your sleight of hand, all these have come to be.

But why this wizardry?

7-8-6

மயக்கா, வாமன்னே! மதியாம் வண்ணம் ஒன்றுளாய்.
அயர்ப்பாய் தேற்றமும் ஆய், அழலாய் குளிராய்
வியப்பாய் வென்றிகளாய் வினையாய் பயனாய் பின்னும் நீ
துயக்காய் நீன்ற வாறிவை என்ன துயரங்களே.

mayakkaa vaamananE! mathiyaam vaNNam onRu aruLaai,
ayarppaai thEtRamumaai azhalaai kuLiraai viyavaai,
viyappaai venRikaLaai vinaiyaai payanaai pinnum nee,
thuyakkaai neendRavaaR ivai enna thuyarangaLE!

Vaamana! Enchanting pygmy!
For heaven's sake put this thing to me
intelligibly.

This lethargy, this lapse of memory:
Is it you? Really?

And strength renewed, and certainty?
The thrills and chills of victory and calamity?

So, you're inevitable Destiny.
This state of being unfree—
it's all you, really.

Why all this misery?

7-8-7

துயரங்கள் செய்யும் கண்ணா! சுடர் நீள் முடியா! அருளாய்.
துயரம் செய் மானங்களாய் மதனாய் உவகைகளாய்
துயரம்செய் காமங்களாய் துலை யாய் நிலயாய் நடையாய்
துயரங்கள் செய்து வைத்தி இவை என்ன சுண்டாயங்களே?

thuyarangaL cheyyum kaNNaa! chudar neeL mudiyaa aruLaai,
thuyaram chei maanangaLaai madhanaai uvakaikaL aai,
thuyaramchei kaamangaLaai thulaiyaai nilai aai nadai aai,
thuyarangaL cheydhuvaithu ivaiyenna chuNtaayangaLE?

Kannaa, you maker of miseries!
You with the flowing, flame-bright hair!
You are grace itself.

But you are too, the shameful agony
that's the doing of the love-god,
who is none other than you.

Yourself.

You become
the afflictions caused by desire,
with their crushing and immoveable weight,
with the restlessness that they create.
It's all your doing.

O, what torments are these?

7-8-8

என்ன சுண்டாயங்களாய் நின்றிட்டாய் என்னை ஆளும் கண்ணா!
இன்னது ஓர் தன்மையை என்று உன்னை யாவர்க்கும் தேற்றறியை
முன்னிய மூவுலகும் அவை ஆய், அவற்றைபடைத்து
பின்னும் உள்ளாய்! புறத்தாய்! இவை என்ன இயற்கைகளே.

enna sundaayangaLaai ninRittaai ennai aaLum kaNNaa,
innathOr thanmaiyai enRu unnai yaavarkkum thEtRariyai,
munniya moovulakum avai aai avaRRai padaiththu,
pinnum uLLaai! puRaththaai! ivai enna iyaRkaikaLE!

As torment and tribulation,
You rule over me, Kannaa.

What you're made of, no one clearly knows.

It was you who made the three worlds.
You became everything in them.
You're within me, and beyond.

What shapes Nature takes!

7-8-9

என்ன இயர்க்கைகளாய் எங்ஙனே நின்றிட்டாய் என் கண்ணா!
துன்னு கரசரணம் முதலாக எல்லா உறுப்பும்
உன்னு சுவை ஒளி ஊறு ஒலி நாற்றம் முற்றும் நீயே.
உன்னை உணரவுறில் உலப்பு இல்லை நுணுக்கங்களே.

enna iyaRkaikaLaal engaNE ninRittaai en kaNNaa,
thunnu karacharaNam muthalaaga ellaa uRuppum
unnu chuvai oLi ooRu oli naaRRam muRRum neeyE,
unnai uNaravuRil ulappu illai nuNukkangaLE.

As Nature's shapes, you're manifest,
my Kannaa, as my very flesh.

From hands and feet to body parts,
taste and light, touch, sound, and smell
in every sense I perceive

your inexhaustible intricacies.

7-8-10

இல்லை நுணுக்கண்களே இதனில் பிறிது என்னும் வண்ணம்
தொல்லை நல் நூலில் சொன்ன உருவும் அருவும் நீயே
அல்லித்துழாய் அலங்கல் அணி மார்ப! என் அச்சுதனே.
வல்லது ஓர் வண்ணம் சொன்னால் அதுவே உனக்கு ஆம் வண்ணமே.

illai nuNukkangaLE idhanil piRithu ennum vaNNam
thollai nal noolil chonna uruvum aruvum neeyE
alli thuzhaai alangGal aNi maarba! en achchuthanE,
vallathu Or vaNNam chonnaal adhuvE unakku aam vaNNamE.

Unravelled, these intricacies
reveal
that all forms are you.
And all that's formless, too,
is you.
Exactly as the good old books have said.

O my imperishable One, with lilies and tulasi
garlanding your handsome chest!

All that is spoken of as 'You'
you are indeed.

7-8-11

ஆம் வண்ணம் இன்னது ஒன்று என்று அறிவது அரிய அரியை
ஆம் வண்ணத்தால் குருகூர்ச் சடகோபன் அறிந்து உறைத்த
ஆம் வண்ண ஒண் தமிழ்கள் இவை ஆயிரத்துள் இப்பத்தும்
ஆம் வண்ணத்தால் உறைப்பார் அமைந்தார் தமக்கு என்றைக்குமே.

aamvaNNam innathu onRu enRu aRivadhariya ariyai,
aamvaNNaththaal kurukoorch chatakOpan aRindhuraiththa
aamvaNNa oN thamizhgaL ivai aayiraththuL ippaththum,
aamvaNNaththaal uraippaar amainNthaar thamakku enRaikkumE.

It's hard to know if Hari is that, or this.
Yet Kurugoor Satakopan, knowing that He exists,
speaks of it in a thousand verses, and these ten more
in sweet Tamil.

Chanting them, those who are aware of
That which Is
will remain forever
in this state of bliss.

7-9-1

என் சொல்லி நிற்ப்பனோ என்னை உய்யக்கொண்டு போகிய
அன்றைக்கு அன்று என்னை தன்னாக்கி என்னால் தன்னை
இன் தமிழ் பாடிய ஈசனை ஆதியை
நின்ற என் சோதியை என்சொல்லி நிற்ப்பனோ?

enRaikkum ennai uyyakkoNdu pOgiya,
anRaikku anRu ennai thannaakki ennaal thannai
in thamizh paadiya eesanai aathiyai-
ninRa en sOthiyai en solli niRppanO?

Forever redeeming me, he carried me away,
made me his own that very day,
in sweetest Tamil sang through me
of his own Self:
Isa, the Origin.

Of this my Light, that always stands by me,
how shall I speak?

How conclude?

7-9-2

என்லொல்லி நிற்பன் என் இன்னுயிரின் ஒன்றாய்
தன் சொல்லால் யான் சொன்ன இங் கவி என்பித்து
தன் சொல்லால் தான் தன்னை கீர்த்தித்த மாயன்
என்முன் சொல்லும் மூவுருவம் முதல்வனே.

en solli niRpan en innuyirin onRaai,
en sollaal yaan chonna inkavi enpiththu,
than sollaal thaan thannaik keerththiththa maayan, en
mun sollum moovuruvam muthalvanE.

How shall I speak, and how conclude
about this One,
who is my own life?

It's he who makes it seem
that what I speak here, in this poem
that's so pleasing to the ear
are my own words.

The Trickster glorifies himself
through these words I speak
which are not mine
but his.
He of the Triune Form,
the First One.

7-9-3

ஆம் முதல்வன் இவன் என்று தன் தேற்றி என்
நா முதல்வந்து புகுந்து நல் இன் கவி
தூமுதல் பத் தற்கு தான் தான் தன்னை சொன்ன என்
வாய் முதல் அப்பனை என்றுமறப்பனோ?

aam muthalvan ivan enRu than thERRi, en
naa muthal vandhu pukundhu nal in kavi
thoomuthal paththarkkuth thaan thannai sonna en
vaai muthal appanai enRu maRappanO?

Yes, he is the First.
Of that he has himself assured me.

Entering my tongue as fine poetry
he has made me sing of him, to those pure ones
who stand first in his worship.

The first word on my lips is 'Father!'
How can I ever forget him?

7-9-4

அப்பனை என்று மறப்பன் என்னாகியே
தப்புதலின்றித் தனைக் கவிதான் சொல்லி
ஒப்பில்லாத்தீவினையேனை உய்யக்கொண்டு
செப்பமே செய்து திரிகின்றசீர் கண்டே?

appanai enRu maRappan ennaagiyE,
thapputhalinR thanaik kavi thaan solli,
oppilaa theevinaiyEnai uyyakkoNdu
cheppamE cheydhu thirikinRa cheer kaNdE?

Can I ever forget my Father,
who became my own self,
and spoke in flawless poetry
of his own Self?

A sinner beyond compare he has redeemed.
Setting me right, straightening me out.

Look how expertly he whirls about!

7-9-11

இங்கும் அங்கும் திருமால் அன்றி இன்மை கண்டு
அங்கணே வண் குர்கூர் சடகோபன்
இங்கணேச் சொன்ன ஓராயிரத்து இப்பத்தும்
எங்கணே சொல்லினும் இன்பம் பயக்குமே.

ingum angum thirumaal anRi inmai kaNdu,
angaNE vaN kurukoorch chatakOpan
ingaNE chonna Or aayiraththu ippaththum
engaNE chollinum inbam payakkumE.

Here or there, without the Sacred Lord,
there's nothing anywhere.
So says the Seer,
Satakopan of Kurugoor.

These thousand and ten verses that he sings here
will bring joy, sung anywhere.

8-1-1

தேவிமார் ஆவார், திருமகள், பூமி, ஏவ மற்று அமரர் ஆட்செய்வார்
மேவிய உலகம் மூன்று அவை ஆட்சி; வேண்டு வேண்டு உருவம் நின் உருவம்
பாவியேன் தன்னை அடுகின்ற கமலக் கண்ணது வாய் பவள மணியே!
ஆவியே! அமுதே! அலை கடல் கடைந்த அப்பனே! காணுமாறு அருளாய்.

dhEvimaar aavaar thirumagaL boomi Eva matRu amarar aatcheivaar
mEviya ulagam moonRu avai aatchi vENdu vENdu uruvam nin uruvam
paaviyEn thannai aduginRa kamalak kaNNadhu vaai pavaLa maNiyE
aaviyE! amudhE! alai kadal kadaindha appanE! kaaNumaaRu aruLaai.

Goddesses are they: Fortune in woman's form, and Earth.
At their behest rule the gods, holding sway over the Three Worlds.
Any form that you desire is yours to assume.
All are images of you.

I'm a sinner, true—but I'm possessed
by you—
those lotus eyes,
those coral lips.
Spirit ambrosial who churned the heaving ocean!
Father, show yourself to me.
Bless me.

8-2-7

*மால் அரி கேசவன் நாரணன் சீமாதவன் கோவிந்தன் வைகுந்தன் என்று என்று
ஓலம் இட என்னை பண்ணிவிடிட்டு ஒன்றும் உருவம் சுவடு காட்டான்;
ஏல மலர்ச்சூழல் அன்னைமீர்காள்; என்னுடை தோழியர்காள் என்
செய்கேன்?
காலம் பல சென்றும் காண்பது ஆணை; உங்களோடு எங்கள் இடை
இல்லையே.*

'maal ari kEsavan naaraNan seemaathavan kOvindhan vaikundhan,'
enRenRu
Olamida ennai paNNivittittu onRum uruvam chuvadu kaattaan.
Elamalar choozhal annaimeergaaL! ennudai thOzhiyarkaaL! en cheikEn?
kaalam pala chenRum kaaNpathu aaNai; ungaLOdu engaL idai illaiyE.

'Great Vishnu!
Hari, Kesavaa, Naaranan,[33] Seemaadhavan, Govindhan, Vaikunthan!'
He's made me call aloud these names and many, many more.
Yet no trace of his form has he shown me.

What then can I do, but let the aeons go by, before
I see Him?
For I have sworn I will.

Ladies with fragrant, flower-bedecked hair, and all my friends, goodbye!
Nothing between us matters any more.

---

[33]Naaranan: a common tamilization of 'Narayanan' (Vishnu). According to the romanization scheme being followed in my transliteration, the first 'N' would be just 'n' and the second 'n' in 'Naaranan' and 'Narayanan' would be the retroflex N. But in my translation itself, I sometimes do not use unfamiliar renditions of Indian words in English, such as capitals in the middle of any word, when it is likely to cause confusion.

...within my reach...

1-9-1

இவையும் அவையும் உவையும் இவரும் அவரும் உவரும்
எவையும் எவரும் தன்னுள்ளே ஆகியும் ஆக்கியும் காக்கும்
அவையுள் தனிமுதல் எம்மான் கண்ணபிரான் என் அமுதம்
சுவையன் திருவின் மண்ணாளன் என்னுடை சூழல் உளானே.

ivaiyum avaiyum uvaiyum ivarum avarum uvarum,
evaiyum yevarum thannuLLE aakiyum aakkiyum kaakkum,
avaiyuL thanimuthal emmaan kaNNabiraan ennamutham
suvaiyan thiruvin maNaaLan ennudai choozhal uLaanE.

This and that, and these and those,
and all other people, and places, and things,
whatever, whichever, whoever they are, they're all
within him.

That's where he becomes them, and it's from
within them
that he shapes and protects them.
For the First One is my own Kannabiraan.
the goddess of fortune's beloved.

He's sweet Immortality
within my reach.

4-5-5

ஆற்ற நல்ல வகை காட்டும் அம்மானை, அமரர் தம்
ஏற்றை எல்லாப் பொருளும் விரித்தானை, எம்மான் தன்னை
மாற்ற மாலை புனைந்து ஏத்தி , நாளும் மகிழ்வு எய்தினேன்.
காற்றின் முன்னம் கடுகி வினை நோய்கள் கரியவே.

aatRa nalla vagai kaattum ammaanai[34] amarar tham
Etrai ellaap poruLum virithaanai, emmaan thannai
maatra maalai punainthu Eththi naaLum makizhvu eithinEn.
kaatrin munnam kadugi vinai nOigaL kariyavE.

Brother, friend, and guide,
he is the one
who shows me what's to be done
and how to do it right.
Great Bull among the gods,
he reveals the meaning
of all things.

Now that I've bedecked him
with this garland of words,
joy shoots up in me each day
in a great gust.
Whatever I've done, or earned
is blown away.
Those maladies are burnt, and turned
to dust.

---

[34]Ammaan, and also emmaan two lines further down: literally, mother's brother. In the Tamil country, this term is used to refer to a close relationship of trust, such as with an elder brother, a mentor, or a friend.

8-1-10

தாள்களை எனக்கே தலை தலை சிறப்பத் தந்த பேர் உதவிக் கைமாறாத்
தோள்களை ஆரத் தழுவி என் உயிரை அற விலை செய் தனன் சோதி
தோள்கள் ஆயிரத்தாய் முடிகள் ஆயிரத்தாய் துணைமலர்க் கண்கள்
ஆயிரத்தாய்!
தாள்கள் ஆயிரத்தாய் பேர்கள் ஆயிரத்தாய் தமியனேன் பெரிய அப்பனே.

thaaLkaLai enakkE thalaiththalai chiRappath thandha pEruthavi
kaimmaaRaa
thOLkaLai aarath thazhuvi en uyirai aRavilai cheitha nanjOthee,
thOLkaL aayiraththaai! mudigaL aayiraththaai thuNai malar kaNkaL
aayiraththaai
thaaLkaL aayiraththaai! pErgaL aayiraththaai! thamiyanEn periya
appanE!

You gave me your feet—a gift beyond price
that stands head and shoulders
above all else.

All I can do in return is to clasp
your shoulders, hold you tight.
Give up my life to your good Light.

O thousand-shouldered, thousand-headed One, with a thousand eyes
like full-blown lotuses!
Of feet, too, you have a thousand, and a thousand names,

O my lord. My Father.

8-1-6

எங்கு வந்துறுகோ என்னை ஆள்வானே? ஏழ் உலகமும் நீயே.
அங்கு அவர்க்கு அமைத்த தெய்வமும் நீ யே. அவற்று அவை கரும முும்
நீயே.
பொங்கிய புறம் பால் பொருள் உளவேலும் அவையுமோ நீ; இன்னே
ஆனால்
மங்கிய அருவாம் நேர்ப்பமும் நீயே; வான் புலன் இறந்தது்தும் நீ யே.

engu vandhu uRugO ennai aaLvaanE Ezh ulagangaLum neeyE
angu avarkku amaiththa dheivamum neeyE avaRRavai karumamum
neeyE
pongiya puRampaal poruL uLavElum avaiyumO nee innE aanaal
mangiya aruvaam nErppamum neeyE vaan pulan iRandhadhum neeyE.

O you who rule over me!
Into which of the seven worlds[35] shall I enter?

You're all of them. You're the gods enthroned in all of them.
And you are, too, everything that those gods do.

Ebullient and bounteous, this world of forms is you.
And when it happens that the haze of formlessness descends
that's you again.

You are the sky, dying, and the death
of every sense.

---

[35]'seven worlds': the seven heavens (svarga loka), which along with the seven hells (patala loka), make up fourteen worlds in Hindu mythological cosmology.

8-7-1

இருத்தும் வியந்து என்னை தன் பொன்னடிக்கீழ் என்று
அருத்தித்து எனைத்து ஓர் பல நாள் அழைதேற்கு
பொருத்தம் உடை வாமனன் தான் புகுந்து என் தன்
கருத்தை உற வீற்றிருந்தான் கண்டு கொண்டே

iruththum viyandhu ennai than ponnadi keezh enRu
aruththiththu enaiththu Or pala naaL azhaithERku
poruththamuda vaamanan thaan pukundhu enthan
karuththai uRa veeRRirundhaan kandukondE.

Holding fast to his feet,
I called out to him, day after day.

Astounded at this evidence
of my persistence,
Vamana shrank himself to a fitting size
and entered me.

It's he who sees to it that I shall have
my say.
He's watching over me.

…being blessed…

8-7-2

இருந்தான் கண்டு கொண்டு எனது ஏழை நெஞ்சு ஆளும்
திருந்தாத ஓர் ஐவரை தேய்ந்து அற மன்னி
பெரும் தாள் களிற்றுக்கு அருள் செய்த பெருமான்
தரும் தான் அருள் தான் இனி யான் அறியேனே.

irundhaan kandukoNdu enathu Ezhai nenju aaLum
thirundhaatha Or aivarai theinthu aRa manni
perum thaaL kaLiRRukku aruL cheitha perumaan
tharum thaan aruL thaan ini yaan aRiyEnE.

Watching over me
he has torn free my poor heart
from the tyranny of the incorrigible
five senses,
that great lord, who once set free
the elephant's foot from the crocodile's jaw.[36]

That I am blessed
is all that I know, now.

---

[36]'…who once set free the elephant's foot/from the crocodile's jaw': a reference to the Puranic legend of the liberation of the elephant-king, Gajendra, by Vishnu from the jaws of a crocodile, Makara.

8-7-3

*அருள் தான் யான் இனி அறியேன், அவன் என் உள்
இருள் தான் அற வீற்றிருந்தான். இது அல்லால்
பொருள் தான் எனில் மூவுலகும் பொருள் அல்ல
மருள் தான் ஈதோ? மாய மயக்கு மயக்கே.*

aruL dhaan ini yaan aRiyEn avan en uL
iruL dhaan aRa veeRRirundhaan ithu allaal
poruL thaan enil moovulagum poruL alla
maruL thaan eethO? maaya mayakku mayakkE.

This feeling
of being blessed
is all I know,
now that he has torn away
the darkness that was in me
and installed
himself.

If it weren't for this feeling
of blessedness
there'd be nothing that makes any sense
in all three worlds.[37]

Or is this thing I'm feeling
a sign of my own
confusion?
Is this delusion?
Is it making me hallucinate?

O bewitching Illusion,
how you fascinate!

---

[37]'three worlds': three states of being—wakefulness, dreaming, and deep sleep.

8-7-4

மாய மயக்கு மயக்கான் என்னை வஞ்சித்து
ஆயன் அமர ர்க்கு அரி ஏறு எனது அம்மான்
தூய சுடர் சோதி தனது என் உள் வைத்தான்
தேயம் திகழும் தன் திருவருள் செய்தே.

maaya mayakku mayakkaan ennai vanchiththu
aayan amararkku ari ERu enathu ammaan
thooya sudar chOthi en uL vaiththaan
dhEyam thigaizhum than thiruvarL cheidhE.

It's Hari himself.
The handsome lion who's lord of the immortals,
that bewitching trickster, has taken me in.
My own Ammaan.

He's close kin.
Planting himself in me
he has set my body alight
with his pure flame.

His blessing.

3-7-9

குலம் தாங்கு சாதிகள் நாலிலும் கீழ் இழிந்து எத்தனை
நலம் தான் இலாது சண்டால சண்டாலர் ஆகிலும்,
வலம் தாங்கு சக்கரத்து அண்ணல் மணி வண்ணர்க்கு ஆள் என்று
உள் கலந்தார் அடியார் தம் அடியார் எம் அடிகளே.

kulam thaangu saathigaL naalilum keezh izhinthu, eththanai
nalam dhaan ilaathu saNdaaLa saNdaaLargaL aakilum,
valam thaangu sakkaraththu aNNal maNivaNNaRkku aaL enRu
uL kalandhaar, adiyaar tham adiyaar em adigaLE.

Born in a lowly family he may be,
among the lowest of the low
in all castes,
or even been
the good-for-nothing that he was before.

Now that he has poured himself
into the heart
of the great lord who wields the Wheel,
he has become his man,
loyal and true.

And not just he,
but his servant's servant is for me
my lord himself, and I
his devotee.

3-6-9

தஞ்சம் ஆகிய தந்தை தாயோடு, தானும் ஆய், அவை அல்லன் ஆய்,
எஞ்சல் இல், அமரர் குலமுதல் மூவர் தம்முள்ளும் ஆதியை
அஞ்சி நீர் உலகத்துள்ளீர்கள்! அவன் இவன் என்று கூழேன்மின்
நெஞ்சினால் நினைப்பான் எவன் அவன் ஆகும் நீள் கடல் வண்ணனே.

thanjam aagiya thanthai thaayodu thaanumaai avai allanaai,
enjal il amarar kula mudhal moovar thammuLLum aathiyaai,
anji neer ulakatthuLLeergaL! avan ivan enRu koozhEnmin
nenjinaal ninaippaan evan avan aagum neeLkadal vaNNanE.

A haven to which you flee,
he's both father and mother.
He is neither, too.

He is your own Self.
Nothing exists apart from him.
He is the Eldest
in the family of the three Immortals.

People of the world!
Don't stammer in terror
that he's 'This!' or 'That!'.
Whoever thinks with his heart,
himself becomes
that One
who is as vast, as blue
as the ocean.

8-7-7

*செவ்வாய் உந்தி வெண் பல் சுடர் க்குழை , தம்மோடு
எவ்வாய் சுடரும் தம்மில் முன் வளாய்க்கொள்ள
செவ்வாய் முருவலோடு எனது உள்ளத்திருந்து
அவ்வாய் அன்றி யான் அறியேன் மற்று அருளே.*

chevvaai undhi veNpal chudarkkuzhai thammOdu
evvaaich chudarum thammil munvaLaaik koLLa
chevvaai muRuvalOdu enadhu uLLaththu irundha
avvaai anRi yaan aRiyEn maRRu aruLE.

Red mouth, flashing white teeth, flowing hair,
O that navel of his!
They vie with one another as he smiles
a rosy smile
here, deep within me.
That mouth is all I know of any state
of blessedness.

8-8-2

அடியேன் உள்ளான் உடல் உள்ளான் அண்டத்து அகத்தான் புறத்துள்ளான்
படியே இது என்று உரைக்கலாம் படியன் அல்லன் பரம்பரன்
கடிசேர் நாற்றத்துள் ஆலை இன் பத் துன்பக் கழி நேர்மை
ஒடியா இன்பப் பெருமை யோன் உணர்வில் உம்பர் ஒருவனே.

adiyEn uLLaan udal uLLaan aNdaththu agaththaan puRaththuLLaan
padiyE ithu enRu uraikkalaam padiyan allan paramparan
kadisEr naaRRaththuL aalai inbath thunbak kazhi nErmai
odiyaa inba perumaiyOn uNarvil umbar oruvanE.

Within this very one, inside this body is he,
the inmost Self
of this world, and of all that lies beyond.

You may declare that this alone is he,
his very measure.
But held down to this or that
or any measure
the lord of all just cannot be.

Infused with a scent
surpassing pain and pleasure
is an unbroken sense
of the Verity.

A jubilant certainty
that above all else is none but
he.

8-8-3

உணர்வில் உம்பர் ஒருவனை அவனது அருளால் உறற்பொருட்டு என்
உணர்வின் உள்ளே இருத்தினேன் அதுவும் அவனது இன் அருளே;
உணர்வும் உயிரும் உடம்பும் மற்று உலப்பிலனவும் பழுதேயும்
உணர்வைப் பெற ஊர்ந்து இற ஏறி யானும் தானாய் ஒழிந்தானே.

uNarvil umbar oruvanai avanadhu aruLaal uRaR poruttu en
uNarvin uLLE iruththinEn athuvum avanathu in aruLE
uNarvum uyirum udambum matRu ulappilanavum pazhudhEyum
uNarvai peRa oornthu iRa ERi yaanum thaanaai ozhindhaanE.

Knowing that in truth, above all else
is none but he,
I fixed him within myself.
That, too, was by his grace.

As the life of the body with all its senses
frayed, decayed, and perished,
I crept up the ladder of knowing,
became my very Self

and vanished.

8-8-4

யானும் தானாய் ஒழிந்தானை யாதும் எவர்க்கும் முன்னோனை
தானும் சிவனும் பிரமனும் ஆகிப் பணைத்த தனி முதலை
தேனும் பாலும் கன்னலும் அமுதம் ஆகி தித்தித்து என்
ஊனில் உயிரில் உணர்வினில் நின்ற ஒன்றை உணர்ந்தேனே.

yaanum thaanaai ozhindhaanai yaathum yevarkkum munnOnai
thaanum sivanum piramanum aagi paNaiththa thani muthalai
thEnum paalum kannalum amuthum aagi thiththiththu
en oonil uyiril uNarvinil ninRa onRai uNarndhEnE.

He who became me
and vanished,
he who was there before anything and anybody else,
he became
Himself, and Siva, and Brahma.
He, the one and only cause of all.

Honey, milk, molasses,
that nectar the immortals feast upon—
he is the sweetness in them.

This thing that stands within
this fleshly body of mine, my life's breath,
my very sense of being—

O, I feel that One!

8-8-5

நின்ற ஒன்றை உணர்ந்தேனுக்கு அதன் நுண் நேர்மை அது இது என்று
ஒன்றும் ஒருவர்க்கு உணரல் ஆகாது உணர்ந்தும் மேலும் காண்பு அரிது
சென்று சென்று பரம் பரம் ஆய் யாதுமின்றி தேய்ந்து அற்று
நன்று தீது அறிவு அரிதாய் நன்றாய் ஞானம் கடந்ததே.

ninRa onRai uNarndhEnukku athan nuN nErmai athu ithu enRu
onRum oruvarkku uNaralaagaadhu uNarndhum mElum kaaNpu arithu
chenRu chenRu param paramaai yaathuminRi thEindhu aRRu
nanRu theethu enRu aRivu aridhaai nanRaai nyaanam kadandhathE.

For anyone who has a sense of that one thing
that's ever present,
to speak of its fine, true essence
as this, or that,
just cannot be.

For it's not a thing that can be known
by anyone.
And even if it were, it can't be seen.

On and on it goes,
becoming greater, ever greater,
till all else is frayed to shreds, and nothing's left.
All sense of good and bad is gone.

All knowledge has been surpassed.

8-8-6

நன்றாய் ஞானம் கடந்த பின் நல் இந்திரியம் எல்லாம் ஈர்த்து
ஒன்றாய் கிடந்த அரும் பெரும் பாழ் உலப்பில் அதனை உணர்ந்து உணர்ந்து
சென்று ஆங்கு இன்பத்துன்பங்கள் செற்று களைந்து பசை அற்றால்
அன்றே அப்போதே வீடு, அதுவே வீடு வீடாமே.

nanRaai nyaanam kadandhupOi nal indhiriyam ellaam eerththu
onRaai kidandha arum perumpaazh ulappil athanai uNarndhu uNarndhu
chenRu aangu inba thunbangaL chetRu kaLaindhu pasai aRRaal
anRE appOthE veedu athuvE veedu veedaamE.

Go well beyond all that's known.
Pull in all the senses at their very best
till you're aware—aware at last—
of what lies out there
all by itself—
the great and formless Deep
where joys and sorrows die, and are thrown off.

If the glue that held them to you
has shriveled up,
that day, at that very moment
you're free.
Free!

That's freedom.

8-8-7

அதுவே வீடு வீடு பேற்று இன்பம் தானும் அது, தேறி
எதுவே தானும் பற்று இன்றி யாதும் இலிகள் ஆகிற்க்கில்
அதுவே வீடு வீடு பேற்று இன்பம் தானும் அது தேறாது
எதுவே வீடு ஏது இன்பம்? என்று எய்தார் எய்தார் எய்தாரே.

adhuvE veedu veedu pERRu inbam thaanum adhu, thERi
edhuvE thaanum paRRu inRi yaadhum iligaL aagiRkil
adhuvE veedu veedu pERRu inbam thaanum adhu thERaathu
edhuvE veedu Edhu inbam? enRu eithaar eithaar eithaarE.

That alone is freedom.
By freedom gained is bliss attained.
When nothing clings to you
no obstacle exists to being free.
That is bliss.

'Freedom? What's that? And what on earth is bliss?'
That's how they scoff, and sneer—
those who haven't made it there.

8-8-8

எய்தார் எய்தார் எய்தாரென்று இல்லத்தாரும் புறத்தாரும்
மொய்து ஆங்கு அலறி முயங்க தாம்போகும் போது
உன்மத்தார் போல் பித்தே ஏறி அனுராகம் பொழியும் போது எம்
பெம்மானோடு
ஒத்தே சென்று அங்குள்ளம் கூடக் கூடிற்றாகில் நல்லுறைப்பே.

eithaar eithaar eithaar enRu illaaththaarum puRaththaarum-
moithu aangu alaRi muyanga thaampOkum pOthu
unmaththar pOl piththE yERi anuraagam pozhiyumpOthu em pemmaanOdu-
oththE chenRu angu uLLamkoodak koodiRRaagil nalluRaippE.

'He's done us, done us, done us in!'
As you depart, your kith and kin
scream, crowd around, fall to the ground.

When that flood of fondness
rises to the very pitch of madness,
get away.
Go alone towards my Lord.

Joining him there, within your heart,
is a trip worth taking, they say.
if you can make it
all that way.

8-8-9

கூடிற்றாகில் நல்லுறைப்புக் கூடாமையைக் கூடினால்
ஆடல் பறவை உயர்கொடி எம் மாயன் ஆவது அதுவே
வீடைப்பண்ணி ஒருபரிசே எதிர்வும் நிகழ்வும் கழிவுமாய்
ஓடித்திரியும் யோகிகளும் உளருமில்லை அல்லரே.

koodiRRaagil nalluRaippu koodaamaiyaik koodinaal
aadal paRavai uyar kodi em maayan aavadhu adhuvE
veedai paNNi oru parisE edhirvum nigazhvum kazhivum aai
Odith thiriyum yOgigaLum uLarumillai allarE.

To strive towards that which seems
beyond your reach is a grand aim,
they claim.
But for the sake of you and me
he, who is that very thing,
becomes the One on whose banner
an eagle soars.

It's all the doing of my lord of miracles.

And that is that—
though there have been, still are,
and always will be
this, or that, or some other yogi
who runs around and stakes a claim
on Freedom.
As though it's some prize they've won in a game.

8-8-10

உளரும் இல்லை அல்லராய் உளராயில்லை ஆகியே
உளர் எம் ஒருவர் அவர் வந்து என் உள்ளத்துள்ளே உறைகின்றார்
வளரும் பிறையும் தேய் பிறையும் போல அசைவும் ஆக்கமும்
வளரும் சுடரும் இருளும் போல் தெருளும் மருளும் மாய்த்தோமே.

uLarum illai allarE uLLaraa illai aagiyE
uLar em oruvar avar vandhu en uLLaththuLLE uRaikinRaar
vaLarum piRaiyum thEi piRaiyum pOla achaivum aakkamum
vaLarum chudarum iruLum pOl theruLum maruLum maaitthOmE.

Whether 'He' is, or it's the contrary,
There is someone. He's mine.
He's come to live here, in me.
The moon waxes, the moon wanes.
Things move, things change.

Like a blazing flame, and night's descent
Are 'clarity' and 'confusion'.
Ah, to both at last I've put an end!

8-8-11

தெருளும் மருளும் மாய்த்து தன் திருந்து செம்பொன் கழல் அடிகீழ்
அருளி இருத்தும் அம்மானாம், அயனாம், சிவனாம் திருமாலால்
அருளப்பட்ட சடகோபன் ஓர் ஆயிரத்துள் இப்பத்தால்
அருளி அடிகீழ் இருத்தும் நம் அண்ணல் கரு மாணிக்கமே.

theruLum maruLum maaiththu thandhirundhu chempon kazhal adi keezh
aruLi iruththum ammaanaam ayanaam sivanaam
thirumaalaal aruLappatta chadakOpan Or aayiraththuL ippaththaal
aruLi adi keezh iruththum namm aNNal karu maaNikkamE.

'Clarity' and 'confusion'
are at an end!

Here, safe and blessed, beneath
the red-gold Feet
of Siva and Brahma and Vishnu, all three,
that dark Gem
who's kinsman, mentor, and friend
Satakopan lays
this decad, one of a thousand.

9-2-3

கிடந்த நாள் கிடந்தாய், எத்தனை காலம் கிடத்தி? உன் திரு உடம்பு அசைய!
குற்றேவல் செய்து தொல் அடிமை வழிவரும் தொண்டரோருக்கு அருளி
தடம் கொள் தாமரை கண்விழித்து நீ எழுந்து உன் தாமரை மங்கையும் நீயும்
இடம் கொள் மூவுலகும் தொழ இருத்தருளாய் திருபுளிங்குடி கிடந்தானே.

kidandha naaL kidandhaai eththanai kaalam kitaththi un thiru udambu achaiya

thodarndhu kutREval seithu thol adimai vazhivarum thondarOrkku aruLi

thadam koL thaamaraikkaN vizhiththu nee ezhundhu un thaamarai mangaiyum neeyum

idangoL moovulagum thozha iruththaruLaai thiru puLingudi kidanthaanE!

How many ages has it been, since the day you fell asleep!
That fine body of yours just lies there, unmoving!

Bestir yourself.
Your devotees await your beck and call.
Like slaves of yore they'll fulfil your slightest whim.
Be kind to them. Arise!
Open those great lotus eyes!

O You who lie in Thirupulingudi.
Take your place beside your Lotus-Woman.
Receive the worship of the Three Worlds.

4-7-6

நோக்கி நோக்கி உன்னை காண்பான் யான் எனது ஆவி உள்ளே
நாக்கு நீள்வான்; ஞானம் இல்லை நாள் தோறும் என்னுடைய
ஆக்கையுள்ளும் ஆவியுள்ளும் அல்ல புறத்தினுள்ளும்
நீக்கம் இன்றி எங்கும் நின்றாய்! நின்னை அறிந்து அறிந்தே.

nOkki nOkki unnai kaaNbaan yaan enadhu aaviyuLLE.
naakku neeLvaan nyaanam illai naaL dhORum ennudaiya
aakkai uLLum aavi uLLum alla puRaththin uLLum
neekkam inRi engum ninRaai! ninnai aRindhu aRindhE.

'I'm looking, I'm looking!' I announced.
'See if I don't see you, in this very life of mine!'
On and on I wagged my tongue.
I knew nothing, then.

When, day after day, in my body, in my breath, in the world outside
nothing remained exempt from your presence,
and there you stood,
everywhere,
I became aware.

I know
I know you now.

9-5-5

அந்தரம் நின்று உழல்கின்ற யானுடைப் பூவைகாள்
நும் திறத்து ஏதும் இடை இல்லை குழறேன் மினோ
இந்திரஞாலங்கள் காட்டி இவ் ஏழ் உலகும் கொண்ட
நம் திரு மார்பன் நம் ஆவி உண்ண நன்கு எண்ணினான்.

andharam ninRu uzhalkinRa yaanudaip poovaikaaL
num thirathu Edhum idai illai kuzhaREn minO
indhira nyaalangaL kaatti ivvEzhulakum konda
nam thirumaarban nam aavi uNNa nangu eNNinaan.

Perched precariously
between earth and sky.
O you birds, don't croon so liquidly!
All your antics and your trilling skills
haven't a leg to stand on,
now that He
has unveiled of sense-delights
whole galaxies.

He of the seven worlds, on whose breast
Beauty herself clings amorously.

He whose intent it is to consume
Our very Being, utterly.

10-10-4

உம்பர் அம் தண் பாழே! ஓ! அதனுள் மிசை நீ யே! ஓ!
அம்பரம் நல் சோதி அதனுள் பிரமன் அரன் நீ.
உம்பரும் யாதவரும் படைத்த முனிவன் அவன் நீ.
எம்பரம் சாதக்கலுற்று என்னை போர விட்டிட்டாயே.

umbar am thaN paazhE! O! athanuLmisai neeyE! O!
ambaram nal jOthi adhanuL biraman aran nee.
umbarum yaathavarum padaiththa munivan avan nee
emparam saathakkaluRRu ennai pOra vitittaayE.

O, blessed firmament on high!
Cold abyss below!
O you who are all that is within.
The sky, the light benign.

Creator and Destroyer.
You, Ancestor and Sage, have made gods, and men.

And yet you've left me to do battle
with this creature,
who's my inborn nature,

all on my own!

7-9-5

சீர் கண்டு கொண்டு திருந்து நல்லிங்கவி
நேர்பட யான் சொல்லும் நீர்மை இலாமையில்
ஏர்வு இலா என்னை தன்னாக்கி என்னால் தன்னை
பார் பரவு இன் கவி பாடும் பரமரே.

cheer kaNdu koNdu thirundhu nal inkavi
nERpada yaan sollum neermai ilaamaiyil
Ervilaa ennaith thannaakki ennaal thannai
paar paravu inkavi paadum paramarE.

He sees the good in me and sets me right.
He makes me speak the finest poetry.
One who lacks fluency, of no high quality
he has made
his own.
And it's through me,
throughout the whole world,
that the Supreme One sings

of himself
in finest poetry.

7-9-7

வைகுந்த நாதன் என் வல் வினைமாய்ந்தறச்
செய்குந்தன்னை என்னாக்கி என்னால் தன்னை
வைகுந்தனாகப் புகழ வன் தீம் கவி
செய்குந்தன் தன்னை என்னால் சிந்தித் ஆர்வனோ?

vaikundha naadhan en valvinai maayndhaRach,
cheikundhan thannai ennaakki ennaal thannai
vaikundhanaaga pukazha van theem kavi,
cheikundhan thannai ennaaL chindhithu aarvanO?

Vaikuntha's Lord has slain my heinous sins,
and made me over into himself!
Vaikuntha's Lord has entered me.
Will I ever cease to wonder
that he chose to praise himself,
through me,
in mighty poetry?

7-9-8

ஆர்வனோ ஆழி அங்கை எம்பிரான் புகழ்
பார்வின் நீர்முற்றும் கலந்துபருகிலும்
ஏர்வில்ல என்னை தன்னாக்கி என்னால் தன்னை
சீர் பெற இன் கவி சொன்ன திறத்துக்கே?

aarvanO aazhi angai empiraan pukazh
paarviN neer muRRum kalandhu parukilum
Ervilaa ennai thannaakki ennaal thannai,
cheer peRa inkavi sonna thiRaththukkE?

Will I ever cease to praise my Lord
whose hand wields the Wheel?
Could I ever drink up the mingled waters
Of all the world's oceans?
Inglorious as I am, he's made me over
into himself.

He's placed within my reach this wealth of words,
and made me sing of Him!

This is all his doing.

7-9-9

திறத்துக்கு எய் துப்புரவு ஆம் திருமாலின் சீர்
இறப்பு எதிர் காலம் பருகிலும் ஆர்வனோ
மறப்பு இலா என்னை தன்னாக்கி என்னால் தன்னை
உறப்பல இன் கவி சொன்ன உதவிக்கே?

thiRaththukku ei thupparavaam thirumaalin seer
iRappu edhir kaalam parukilum aarvanO?
maRappilaa ennaith thannaakki ennaal thannai,
uRappala inkavi sonna uthavikkE?

This wealth of words is his, it's all his doing!
Were I to swallow death itself,
and all that is to be,
would it ever cease
to amaze me
that he took over
this dull self of mine,

made me speak
of his own Self
in fine poetry?

…trapped in debt…

7-9-10

உதவிக்கை மாறு என்னுயிர் என்ன உற்று எண்ணில்
அதுவும் மாற்றாங்கவன் தன்னது என்னால் தன்னை
பதவிய இன் கவி பாடிய அப்பனுக்கு
எதுவும் ஒன்றும் இல்லை செய்து இங்கும் அங்கே.

udhavik kaimmaaRu ennuyir enna uRRu eNNil,
adhuvum maatRaangavan thannadhu ennaal thannai,
padhaviya inkavi paadiya appanukku
edhuvum onRumillai cheyvadhu ingum angE.

How shall I repay him for what he's done for me?
My life's already his.
For my Father who has made me sing of him
in fine poetry,

there's nothing I can ever do—
here or there
or anywhere.

4-9-8

காட்டி நீ கரந்து உமிழும் நிலம் நீர் தீ வுசும்பு கால்
ஈட்டி நீ வைத்து அமைத்த இமையோர் வாழ் தனி முட்டை
கோட்டையினில் கழித்து என்னை உன் கொழும் சோதி உயரத்து
கூட்டு அரிய திருவடிக்கள் எஞ்ஞான்றும் கூட்டுதியே?

kaattinNee karandhu umizhum nilam neer thee visumbu kaal,
eetti nee vaiththu amaiththa imaiyOrvaazh thanimuttaik,
kOttaiyinil kazhiththu ennai un kozhum chOthi uyaraththu
koottu ariya thiruvadikkaL ennyaanRum koottudhiyE?

You have shown me all
that you've spewn out.
This peerless Sphere, this Egg, all-encompassing,
that you have wrought,
abode and fortress of the ever-wakeful gods.

I've done my time here. Set me free!
Lift me to that Light pristine, above.

Or must your Feet be forever
far
from me?

4-9-10

கண்டு, கேட்டு உற்று, மோந்து உண்டு உழலும் ஐங்கருவி
கண்ட இன்பம், தெரிவு அரிய அளவு இல்லாச்சிற்றின்பம்
ஒண்தொடியாள் திருமகளும் நீயுமே நிலா நிற்ப
கண்ட சதிர் கண்டொழிந்தேன்; அடைந்தேன் உன் திருவடியே.

kandukEttu uRRu mOndhu undu uzhalum aingaruvi
kanda inbam, therivu ariya aLavillaach chitRinbam,
oNdhodiyaaL thirumagaLum neeyumE nilaa niRpa,
kanda sadhir kandozhindhEn adaindhEn un thiruvadiyE.

I gazed and heard, felt, smelt, and swallowed
all that the five senses offered.
And while I wallowed in earthly pleasure
beyond all measure,
there she stood, bejewelled,
beside you.

Beholding the dance
that the two of you do
I fell into a trance, was lost and gone,
and found myself here,
at your feet.

...release.

1-1-7

thida visumbu eri vaLi neer nilam ivai misai
padar poruL muzhuvadhum aai avai avaidhoRum
udal misai uyirenak karandhu engum parandhuLan
sudar miku suruthiyuL ivai unda suranE.

thida visumbu eri vaLi neer nilam ivai misai
padar poruL muzhuvadhum aai avai avaidhoRum
udal misai uyirenak karandhu engum parandhuLan
sudar miku suruthiyuL ivai unda suranE.

Firmament and fire, air, water, earth—
the substance that pervades each
subsumes them all.

Like life coiled in the body's pit, swelling up and snaking out,
revelation blazes up within.

O Being, who consumes them all!

4-9-9

கூட்டுதி நின் குரை குழல்கள்; இமையோரும் தொழாவகை செய்து
ஆட்டுதி நீ; அரவு அணையாய்! அடியேனும் அ .. து அறிவன்.
வேட்கை எல்லாம் விடுத்து என்னை உன் திருவடியே சுமந்து உழலக்
கூட்டு அரிய திருவடிக்கள் கூட்டினை நான் கண்டேனே.

koottudhi nin kuraikazhalgaL imaiyOrum thozhaavagai seidhu,
aattudhi nee aravaNaiyaai! adiyEnum ahadhu aRivan,
vEtkaiyellaam viduththu ennai un thiruvadiyE sumandhu uzhala,
koottariya thiruvadikkaL koottinai naan kandEnE.

That you have made your feet hard to reach
for the ever-wakeful gods themselves
even I know, as I lie here
at those very feet.

O you, lying on that snake!
You've stripped me of all my hankerings,
made me roam around, weighed down
by these fine Feet of yours
that are so very hard
to reach....

It's as though those feet of yours
are part of me....

Ah! I see it now.
Your Feet
are
Mine.

5-2-1

பொலிக பொலிக பொலிக போயிற்று வல் உயிர் சாபம்.
நலியும் நரகமும் நைந்த நமனுக்கு இங்கு யாதொன்றும் இல்லை
கலியும் கேடும் கண்டு கொண்மின் கடல் வண்ணன் பூதங்கள் மண்மேல்
மலிய புகுந்து இசை பாடி ஆடி உழிதரக்கண்டோம்.

poliga poliga poliga! pOyitRu val uyir chaabam
naliyum naragamum naindha namanukku ingu yaadhonRum illai
kaliyum kEdum kandu koLmin kadalvaNNan boodhangaL maN mEl
maliya pugundhu isaipaadi aadi uzhidharak kandOm.

Light!
Blazing, glorious light!
It's gone—the curse upon this cruel life.
Hell's wasting woes,
death's throes—
there's nothing left of all that here.

Look, the aeon's[38] ills are over!
Blue as the sea,
he flows into all the elements
upon the earth,
sings, dances, roves about.

Here, there, everywhere
he's the one
we see.

---

[38]Kali Yuga: the present age, characterized by evil, discord, and calamities. It is the fourth and last in a recurring cycle of ages mentioned in ancient texts, one being the Bhagavata Purana.

5-2-4

இடம் கொள் சமயத்தை எல்லாம் எடுத்துக் களைவன போலே
தடங்கடல் பள்ளிப் பெருமான் தன்னுடை பூதங்களே ஆய்
கிடந்தும் இருந்தும் எழுந்தும் கீதம் பலபல பாடி
நடந்தும் பரந்தும் குனித்தும் நாடகம் செய்கின்றனவே.

idam koL samayaththai ellaam eduththuk kaLaivana pOlE
thadan kadal paLLip perumaan thannudai boodhangaLE aai
kidandhum irundhum ezhundhum geetham palapala paadi
nadandhum paRandhum kuniththum naadagam seiginRanavE.

Gone are all the isms that were here before!
Those ideologies and schisms are now
no more.
They've been cleared out and whisked away.

Embedded in Being's heaving ocean
the Great One has become
his own elements.
They are all that's here—
everything that lies inert,
sits quiet, stands alert.

It's they who walk about,
who soar,
who dance and sing melodies galore.
They're the actors

in this play.

2-9-6

*மகிழ் கொள் தெய்வம் உலோகம் அலோகம்
மகிழ் கொள் சோதி மலர்ந்த அம்மானே
மகிழ்கொள் சிந்தை சொல் செய்கை கொண்டு என்றும்
மகிழ்வுற்று உன்னை வணங்க வாராயே.*

magizh koL dheivam ulOkam alOkam,
magizh koL chOdhi malarndha ammaanE,
magizhkoL sindhai sol seikai kondu, enRum
magizhvutRu unnai vaNanga vaaraayE.

Ammaan![39]
You're the joy in this world
and in the other too.
You blossom as delight, and illumine
all that I think, and say, and do.

You've made me rejoice forever
in your worship.

You've come to me.

---

[39]'Ammaan': literally mother's brother (sometimes, as in 1-9-1, 'emmaan' meaning 'my own maternal uncle'). This appellation expresses the closeness of the bond with God, in some ways closer than Appan or Father. The relationship with one's mother's brother is highly valued in Tamil society, the maternal uncle being a trusted companion, often a mentor, and sometimes, with first-cousin marriages, a man's father-in-law. It used to be common that a girl's mother's younger brother marries her. This term just cannot be rendered as 'uncle' in English.

9-4-8

உரு ஆகிய ஆறு சமயங்கட்கு எல்லாம்
பொரு ஆகி நின்றான் அவன் எல்லா பொருட்கும்
அரு ஆகிய ஆதியை தேவர்கட்கு எல்லாம்
கரு ஆகிய கண்ணனை கண்டு கொண்டேனே.

uru aagiya aaRu samayangatku ellaam
poru aagi ninRaan avan ellaa porutkum
aru aagiya aadhiyai dhEvargatkellaam
karu aagiya kaNNanai kandu koNdEnE.

There he stands,
in the six 'Ways of Seeing'.[40]

It's he who has given to each vision
its substance and significance.
His is the subtle essence which transcends
all things.
He is the Origin.

That unborn Child of the gods
is the Kannan I see.

I've found him.

---

[40] 'Ways of Seeing': the Darshanas, six philosophical systems based on the Vedas—Sankhya, Yoga, Nyaya, Vaisheshika, Mimamsa, and Vedanta.

2-3-2

ஒத்தார் மிக்காரை இலையாய மா மாயா!
ஒத்தாய் எப்பொருட்கும் உயிர் ஆய் என்னை பெற்ற
அத் தாய் ஆய், தந்தை ஆய், அறியாதன அறிவித்து
அத்தா! நீ செய்தன அடியேன் அறியேனே.

oththaar mikkaarai ilaiyaai maa maayaa!
oththaai epporutkum uyir aai ennai petRa
ath thaai aai, thanthai aai aRiyaathana aRiviththu
aththaa[41]! nee seithana adiyEn aRiyEnE.

Grand master!
In this your wizardry
you have no match.
None can even come up to scratch
let alone better you
at this game.

You became
the one breath in all things.
You became
the mother who gave birth to me.
You became my father, too.
O friend!
What's more,
it's you who've made me know
what I never knew before.
All that you have done,
I, who lie here at your feet,

do not know.

---

[41] *அத்தா*, aththaa: shortened form of 'aththaan', an uncle's son, or one's brother-in-law. An 'aththaan' is close kin, used to address a trusted friend.

1-1-2

மனன் அகம் மலம் அற மலர் மிசை எழுதரும்
மன ன் உணர்வு அளவு இலன், பொறி உணர்வு அவை இலன்
இன ன் உணர்வு முழு நலம் எதிர் நிகழ் கழிவினும்
இன ன் இலன் என ன் உயிர் மிகு நறை இலனே.

manan akam malam aRa malar misai ezhudharum
manan uNar vaLavu ilan poRi uNarvu avai ilan
inan uNarvu, muzhu nalam edhir nigazh kazhivinum
inan ilan enan uyir migu narai ilanE.

Stripped of dross, both mind and inmost self
blossom and ripen.
Beyond the mind's measure and the senses' grasp
always and forever, is a perfect wholeness.

Nothing and no one excels the matchless
life within.

1-2-7

அடங்கு எழில் சம்பத்து
அடங்க கண்டு ஈசன்
அடங்கு எழில் அ .. து என்று
அடங்குக உள்ளே.

adangu ezhil sampaththu
adanga kandu eesan
adangu ezhil ahadhu enRu
adanguka uLLE.

Steeped in beauty is the treasure that is Isa.
Look within.
Take a plunge into that glory.
Dive right in.

2-9-9

யானே என்னை அறியலாகாதே
யானே என் தனதே என்றிருந்தேன்
யானே நீ என் உடைமையும் நீயே
வானையேத்தும் எம் வானவர் ஏறே.

yaanE ennai aRiyagilaathE
yaanE en thanadhE enRu irundhEn
yaanE nee en udaimaiyum neeyE.
vaanai yEththum em vaanavar ERE.

Unknown to me was my own self.
I took it to be mine alone—
this 'my own self'.

But I am you.
Everything I own is you.

You hold up the sky.
You set it aflame.

O mighty lord of heavenly beings.

…And revelation.

1-10-2

*கண்ணுள்ளே நிற்க்கும் காதன்மையால் தொழில்
எண்ணிலும் வரும்; என் இனி வேண்டுவம்?
மண்ணும் நீரும் எரியும் நல் வாயுவும்
விண்ணும் ஆய் விரியும் என் பிரானையே.*

kaNNuLLE niRkkum kaadhanmaiyaal thozhil
eNNilum varum, en ini vEnduvam?
maNNum neerum eriyum nal vaayuvum,
viNNum aai viriyum empiraanaiyE.

Behind my eyes love stands watch.
Even in thoughts of worldly business
love shows up.

What more could I desire?

Earth, water, fire,
the blessed air, the sky above—
my lord becomes all these
and spreads beyond.

Acknowledgements

Among those who have helped me stay on track and bring out this book are the following four persons whom I thank deeply for their critical inputs.

Sita Anantha Raman is Emerita Associate Professor of South and Southeast Asian History at Santa Clara University. A PhD in South and Southeast Asian History from the University of California, Los Angeles, she worked with historian and Indologist Dr Stanley Wolpert. Apart from articles and monographs on social reform movements and women's education in India, her major publications include *Women's Rights and Law Codes in Early India, 600 BCE–570 ACE* (2020), *Women in India: A Social and Cultural History* (2 volumes, 2009), *Getting Girls to School: Social Reform in the Tamil Districts, 1870–1930* (1996), and *A. Madhaviah: A Biography and a Novella* (translated from Tamil by Vasantha Surya, 2004).

Mini Krishnan has promoted translations from Indian literature into English for almost three decades. Beginning as one of the sixteen chief editors under K. M. George of the two-volume collection brought out by the Kerala Sahitya Akademi and Macmillan India, *Comparative Indian Literature*, she has since edited thirty-seven translations of ancient, medieval, and contemporary Indian literature for Macmillan India and seventy-two for Oxford University Press.

A founding editor of the South Asia Website for Women Writers hosted by the British Council, she is a member of the Translation Mission and Indian Literature Abroad. Having served as consultant editor of the translation programme of the Thunchath Ezhuthachan Malayalam University, Tirur, she is now co-ordinating editor of the Tamil Nadu Textbook Corporation's Tamil–English translation programme.

David Dean Shulman is an Emeritus Professor at the Hebrew University at Jerusalem who moved to Israel in the late sixties. His has been a lifelong pursuit of scholarship and proficiency in several languages, including Hebrew, Arabic, Persian, Turkish, Greek, Russian, Sanskrit, Hindi, Telugu, and Tamil. He has a PhD in Tamil and Sanskrit from the School of Oriental and African Studies at the University of London. His books include *More than Real: A History of the Imagination in South India*, and *Tamil: A Biography*. In an interview with Daniel Bezelel Richardsen of *Tablet*, Shulman has described his experience of Tamil as 'love at first sight', comparing the language to 'the rapid rushing of a rivulet…a delicious, bewitching, incantational music, unlike any other that I have heard.' This multilingual savant is a peace activist supporting Ta'ayush, a joint Israeli–Palestinian peace movement.

Nanjamma Chinnappa moved on from a career as a statistical consultant to the translation and documentation of the language, folklore, and culture of the Kodagu region. She and her husband, Boverianda M. Chinnappa, are co-authors of an English translation (2003) of Nadikerianda Chinnappa's 1924 compilation *Pattole Palame* on Kodava culture, folksongs, and traditions, shortly to appear as a bilingual edition, and *Ainmanes of Kodagu* (2014), a study of the ancestral homes of Kodagu. As editors and contributors, they have assisted B. C. Uthaiah and B. U. Thangamma in compiling *Arivole* (2016), a trilingual dictionary of the Kodava language.

Rupa
1148
16/5/22